WINGWALKING

By the same author
The Confessional Fictions of Charles Dickens
The Fairchild Family (ed.)

WINGWALKING

BARRY WESTBURG

SIRIUS

All characters in this book are
entirely fictitious, and no reference
is intended to any living person.

Promotion of this title has been assisted
by the South Australian Government
through the Department for the Arts.

Creative writing programme assisted by the
Literature Board of the Australia Council,
the Federal Government's arts funding
and advisory body.

ANGUS & ROBERTSON PUBLISHERS

Unit 4, Eden Park, 31 Waterloo Road,
North Ryde, NSW, Australia 2113, and
16 Golden Square, London W1R 4BN,
United Kingdom

First published in Australia
by Angus & Robertson Publishers in 1988

National Library of Australia
Cataloguing-in-publication data.

Westburg, Barry, 1938–
    Wingwalking and other tales.
    ISBN 0 207 15598 4.
    I. Title.
813'.54

Typeset in 11 pt Bembo by Midland
Printed in Hong Kong

*In memory
of Richard Westburg*

ACKNOWLEDGEMENTS

First off, I'd like to thank Glenda Adams for her initial encouragement. Thanks also to Peter, Prue, Beate, Jeri, David and Andrew, who have offered me a lot of helpful criticism over the past few years. And thanks, finally, to a street, Friendly Street, Adelaide, where some of these tales were read to a heckling roomful of wine-drinking lovers of *le mot juste*.

I must apologise to Julia, my most faithful critic, for my never having put her into a story. The truth is, none of my characters — including the narrators — should be mistaken for real people.

Finally, I'd like to thank the following publications, in whose pages some of these stories have appeared: *The Australian Literary Magazine; The Australian Bedside Book* (Macmillan Australia, edited by Geoffrey Dutton); *Overland; Northern Perspective; Quadrant; Coast to Coast* (Angus & Robertson Publishers, edited by Kerryn Goldsworthy); *Adelaide Review; Island Magazine; Unsettled Areas* (Wakefield Press, edited by Andrew Taylor); *Australian Short Stories.*

BW
Adelaide, South Australia

CONTENTS

Contents

WINGWALKING

Let me be frank. I don't want to tell this story. I'm afraid it doesn't reflect very well on myself . . . or on my father. It concerns the time my father tried to establish my brother and me in a useful trade. Unfortunately the trade he chose to initiate his two sons into was — wingwalking.

"Wingwalking?"

Correct.

"You mean, like, uh . . . walking on the wings of an airplane?"

Uh-huh, particularly when it's in flight, at around five thousand feet or so. But — normally — nothing to worry about much! You use a slow old biplane, with lots of struts and things to hang on to.

You've got to understand the context. Just after World War II ended, the Midwest of the United States was crawling with fanatics of all descriptions. But certain fanatics were inflamed by something technological that was just coming on, they were crazy about *flight*. In the late 'thirties the craze was airplane racing. Then, come the late 'forties, it was stunt flying, and gee-whiz airshows. We had one in Des Moines about every month or so.

Maybe your family goes to the beach for the weekend, or maybe you play a little football. Well, my family would be out at the local "field" by dawn, and we'd all be tinkering with aircraft and taking them up for "spins".

Cessnas? Piper Cubs? — those were for the impossibly wealthy, or the expense-account businessmen with corn-meal mush instead of poetry in their veins. Our planes — namely, the planes flown by our hordes of suicidal enthusiasts — came in outrageous shapes and sizes. They were mostly locally designed and assembled and bore unique brand names.

You see, another symptom of the flight fever of the times was the springing-up, all over the Midwest, of colleges of "aeronautical engineering". These were about as common as Kentucky Fried Chicken franchises are now. "Farley/Pratt Institute of Aeronautical Engineering", "Curtis/Starkweather Flight Institute", "McCubbins Aeronautical College", and so on. Most of them were shopfronts with a patch of landing strip behind. Usually a couple of planes partly assembled would be out there in a shed — the "hangar". These were being built as student projects. It was like doing a thesis, except that you had to *fly* the completed project before you were awarded your BA in "aeronautical engineering". In special cases, posthumous degrees could be earned.

My father's buddy, "Buzz" Curtis, who had gone through most of the war with him, took his GI Loan and founded the "North American Aeronautical Institute", which was a couple of sheds behind a subsidiary taxi-strip of the Des Moines airport. That's where we picked up our own family biplane. The price tag was a steep five hundred bucks, but the idea was that we could paint it ourselves...and of course do the "air-testing" — the "North American Chickenhawk" had never been taken up. The neurotic genius who designed it had dropped out of college, so a few first-year students were trying to finish it for him, following as closely as possible the absinthe-stained sketches left on his drawing board. This stormy petrel of aeronautics had in fact migrated to Paris, to join the flocks of poets and writers who were presumed to be roosting in exile there. Paris, Ohio, I mean. He was woefully off course.

We took delivery of the North American Chickenhawk as soon as it was finished (or very nearly so). Buzz Curtis towed it over to my father's hangar behind a reconverted International Harvester threshing machine. My father paid him three hundred dollars on the spot and gave him one of his characteristic post-dated checks for another seventy-five.

In those days, the disease of flight had infected even our names. Everybody had an onomatopoetic nickname like "Buzz" or "Speed" and the common form of greeting was "Hey-y-y, Ace!" Even though I didn't learn to fly until I was eight or nine or so, I affected many of the mannerisms of airshow fliers who, in those times of peace, were the true knights of the air. You had to wear your hair long, creating a mane effect, which could then be "windblown". I wanted to change my name to "Buzz", or at least to "Chazz", but this met with resistance from my mother who claimed to have taken pains in choosing my original name. But my given name (Norbert) seemed woefully lacking in heroic overtones. My brother's name — Ron — seemed to have the proper flier's ring to it.

My father's hangar, truth to tell, was the property of the US Air Force. Because he was the leader of the local Air National Guard Squadron he felt entitled to park the North American Chickenhawk alongside the Dauntlesses, the Corsairs, the Mustangs, the Thunderbolts — all the obsolescent fighter planes we spent our waking hours tuning up and flying.

So the Chickenhawk arrives and we finish her up, painting her an autumnal pumpkin colour. (Rather like the camouflage on the old World War I English Spads, which she vaguely resembled — her designing genius was, in respect to bodyline, a kind of aeronautical Tory.) Then one gusty afternoon the old man takes her up and tries every stunt in the book with her, just testing her out. She does most things a plane can do in the air, but not without feminine protest:

3

she squeals, spits, hisses — with sometimes an eerie, eldritch sigh. For she is something of a Frankenstein's Bride among airplanes, built up out of several generations of spare parts. She's neither a lass nor a hag, but a little of each.

Next the old man (actually he's not yet thirty) takes Ron and me up in her and we fly over the farmlands, upside down, for half an hour or so to see if, with added payload, anything will shake loose, as all the groaning struts portend. We fly over my grandfather's original homestead — a haunted, scenic place now known as Devil's Backbone State Park. My Great-aunt Kate Newberry's old house is still down there, three storeys high, Victorian style, where she still keeps three of four "girls", including — of most interest to us boys — a cook.

We fly over at an altitude of about five hundred feet, still upside down, and spot the cook herself, a black woman who looks like the original Aunt Jemima. She's on her way to the chickenhouse to wring a few necks for dinner. We whiz past, eighty miles an hour, upside down, fanning our ears and thumbing our noses. With a stuck-pig squeal she runs for her mistress. She knows the reaction we want. Our first mission seems somehow . . . accomplished.

And so, if *flight* was the thing now, perhaps *beyond* flight was — wingwalking. "You boys will have to do something to *distinguish* yourselves," the old man said. "We'll have to do something at the airshows that nobody else has the *guts* to do. Something that takes skill, too, because any jerk can risk his life. It's *how* you risk it that makes other people take notice of you."

My brother and I — or at least I — pondered this wisdom (sententious, like all parental utterances in America) though we knew that once Dad had made up his mind there was no arguing. Nothing could save you from one of my father's schemes if he thought it would combine profit with education.

And, by the way, why was it good to have folks "take notice" of you? Why should you *want* folks to take notice of you? My father assumed that life was all display and competition. It was not until we heard the wingwalking proposal that we (or I) began to question certain of the old man's — uh — values.

All this brings me back to Ron and me and the awful burden that was being strapped on us by a father who had spent a life of hair-raising adventure — including some three military and two civilian plane crashes — in a state of perpetual (and some would say maniacal) cheerfulness.

Ron was always his willing slave, as a nine-year-old who has formed few lasting opinions can be. But I was a year older and beginning to question the old man. This caused acute embarrassment to Ron, who was coming to regard me as a monster of filial impropriety.

The day we were to begin wingwalking was in August. The seasonal hurricanes would hopefully not give us too much trouble. There was just the oppressive humidity to deal with, but once we got aloft in the North American Chickenhawk this would not bother us quite so much. I have a tendency to perspire easily even in the calmest of circumstances but I was soaked with sweat when we took off. Even though the open cockpits exposed us to a comfortable airflow, the sweat was still whipping off my flier's mane into my kid brother's windburned face.

Prior to takeoff each of us had been tossed a little chute-pack by the old man — but contemptuously. A chute was a useless prophylaxis. What *danger* was there? What danger, for chrissake, *could* there be?

Thus Dad scorned showing us how to use it. Come the crunch, any intuitive boy would be able to figure out which cord to pull (there were three or four cords in a tangle). And any boy of *his*!... well! And so he idly flipped us the chute-packs — which he had picked up at an army surplus sale. He had never tested them anyway.

Lighting one of his beloved Churchillian stogies he said that all the air force had to do was to find "one moth in a warehouse" and they would condemn the entire contents. That's how come the chutes were sold so cheaply (to be used for making curtains and pinafores and the like) and that is why they had stamped on them: CONDEMNED.

With that word on our backs Ron and I took off, with Dad up forward at the controls. It was heartening to recall that Dad had never had to bail out in any of his mishaps. He had always gone down with the ship and hobbled away with — hardly — a scratch.

Dad would turn around every few minutes and shout instructions, but he might as well have been in a silent movie. His hand gestures were easier to read but still ambiguous, perhaps because he was also waving his cigar. The blowing ashes (as usual) were scorching our eyes but we got used to that when we travelled with him, be it by car, train, speedboat or balloon.

He had as yet no finalised plan as to how we would stage the actual, definitive wingwalking. He would work it out during the climb to five thousand feet and announce the details once we made our . . . uh . . . rendezvous.

"Rendezvous?"

Well, yes . . . Buzz Curtis was going to take up his cropduster (a plane of similar pedigree to the North American Chickenhawk) and "rendezvous" with us directly over Des Moines. My father was no conscious symbolist but the exact point of rendezvous was to be over the Equitable Life Assurance Society offices, the highest building in Iowa (ten storeys). We would then fly in a triangular path using the Swedish Cemetery and Mercy Hospital as our points of reference.

What we were supposed to do, as I say, was not worked out in detail, since we were doing something relatively novel, for which the script had not been written — yet.

So now we see a biplane with a redheaded, woody-woodpeckerish man flying it. My father waves his cigar, again showering his sons with hot ashes. Buzz waves back and clasps his hands vigorously over his head — the old salute. Dad starts giving us orders then. He turns and points at one of us, but I decide he means Ron, not me. He shakes his head and points again. Age before beauty? Perhaps he does mean me, but I play Dopey the Dwarf for a few more seconds. He shakes his head disgustedly and points and shouts again. This time Ron stands up. Okay, okay the old man seems to be saying. Ron points his finger at his chest: "Me, Dad, is it me you want, huh? huh?" Moving like an octogenarian my kid brother stands up in his seat. We take a few spar-shuddering turns over Mercy Hospital with Ron still standing, trying to balance himself. Then, at a further shouted (but still ambiguous) command, Ron gingerly puts his right leg out of the cockpit. Buzz and my father grin tolerantly at this tentativeness in the young, who are so inexperienced in doom.

Within a few minutes Ron is clear out on the wing. He turns and shrugs, awaiting further instructions.

At this point I am trying to hand Ron the chute, which, in his haste to be obliging, he has left behind him in the cockpit. Ron is a bit too far out on the wing by now to retrieve the chute easily, unless...unless *I* am willing to take it out to him. I wave it at him, trying to coax him to come and fetch it. I remain seated all the while. It is clear he will have to come all the way back down the wing to get the chute and, what with the picking up of the wind (the usual harbinger of the hurricane front), to do this now seems even more of a bother than just going on without the chute.

Ron still doesn't cotton on: WHAT AM I S'POSED TO DO? (he's out near the wing tip) so he tries a few tentative gymnastics and dance steps. His shifting weight keeps us dipping and swerving to trim the craft, but in a little while we get the knack of making adjustments for that unpredictable moving weight out on the wing tip. We never know what he will try next. Charleston, jig... half-gainer?

Now Buzz moves his craft into position, tip to tip with the North American Chickenhawk. This is rather hard to do with the increasing gusts of the hurricane front buffeting us, but Buzz manages to close the gap to six or eight feet or so, which seems like enough space for Ron's final stunt. The old man winks at his old buddy and gives his boy the high sign.

And...uh...then...

"And then *what*, for chrissakes?"

Well, what do *you* think happens?

SILVER EARRINGS IN COLORADO

In our observation of the world around us we are continually discovering *relationships* among the things that are familiar to us. For example, we notice that old jacaranda trees can be short while young ones can be tall. That people with big noses might pay high taxes while people with small bums might pay no taxes at all. That the postage required for a letter might be determined by the weight of the postman. That a baseball thrown into the air rises to a height proportionate to the integrity of somebody's grandmother. That the price of an article is determined by the venue of sale. That the tangent of an angle depends on the mood of the angler.

Today, I'm rather reflective.

My thoughts have been returning to my birthplace, the Northern Hemisphere. The Northern Hemisphere invented deep thoughts: if we have any deep thoughts here in the sleepy Southern Hemisphere, it is because they have been imported.

For instance, how many great Fijian philosophers or scientists have there been? I can think of only one Fijian Reflective and that is my old friend Carbon Man.

And Carbon Man got that way after we took a little trip up North together, travelling on my credit cards.

We started out in Cambridge, Massachusetts, with the intention of following the old wagon trail to the West Coast, and so to end up in my birthplace, San Francisco. We started out the very night we struck set at the Loeb Theatre in Cambridge, where we had been playing in *The Resistible Rise of Arturo Ui*. I had played Ui. Carbon Man played my henchperson, Rosenblatt. Not an incongruous bit of casting: Carbon Man was a terrific gunman. At one point he would jump down into the audience and fire several blank cartridges into the faces of bejewelled dowagers — to great effect. When we were doing *All the King's Men* the week before, Carbon Man was cast as Sugar Boy, another gunman, this time one with a stutter. He developed a terrific stutter, which wouldn't let go. He still has it. I of course played the lead once again, though I forget the name of the character at this moment. I had been the stand-in for my friend Brad, who died of a stroke on stage during dress rehearsal.

My kid brother Marc had driven from California for the occasion in a racked-up Pinto. He had picked up Mandy and Gary in upstate New York. And so we all set out for the West. Carbon Man had borrowed an old Caddy convertible from a girlfriend and he followed us. He can easily pass for a Chicano in the North, which gives him a certain mileage as a Latin Loverboy type. To support this mild deception he had teamed up with a guy named Ricardo Corrado who was genuine Mexican and they would find a lot of common interests: Anglo women, primarily. And, eventually, deep philosophy.

Every time our little caravan got to a rest stop on the endless turnpikes of the East and freeways of the Midwest we would permutate the seating arrangements, Gary and Mandy and Ricardo floating from car to car as the whim moved them.

Mandy and Gary were married but getting ready to split up; this was to be their last trip together. Gary a geologist wanting to see the Great Divide and especially the Rockies where they begin in

Eastern Colorado. Mandy eager to explore the silver mines up in Cripple Creek. So our initial objective was Colorado.

Ricardo, smoking his Montecristo panatella, didn't care where he was going so long as it was conducive to deep philosophy and shallow Anglo women.

At this time, possession of a Montecristo (Havana, Cuba) cigar was more serious than possession of marijuana or heroin. Try getting one in over the Canadian border! It makes a nice little experiment for a would-be revolutionary.

I had smoked them, but like a snivelling coward I went to Canada to do it. This was some years before Carbon Man and the plays in Cambridge: several of us were up in Ottawa on the Peck Farm. That was a Poetical Farming Experience. In fact my kid brother Marc wrote a few poems about it, which were later published in the *Atlantic Monthly* (May 1977).

Up at Peck Farm we got a sampling of the simple non-urban earthbound sunsoaked life. We got the hay in our hair. We went up as a favour to my old friend Doctor Peck, who wanted to lounge about in Majorca (or was it Minorca?) and to forget about his cows and chickens along the Bonnechere River in the lush Ottawa River valley.

This was when my third wife Madge was still with us and hadn't freaked out and turned into a bitch and thereafter a slut. Sluttishness was in her blood and the taint of it began to show under the stress of primitive earthbound sunsoaked poetical farming conditions. Actually all that we did there was to sit on the banks of the beautiful Bonnechere River drinking Jack Daniels Black Label and target-shooting with a .22 rifle and feeding the livestock — we didn't do any farming — I'm still not even sure what farming is. *And* talking a lot of deep philosophy.

And so we would all sit around and smoke those forbidden Montecristo panatellas until we were green in the gills.

At night the local beavers would topple the local trees and chew them up and pile them into beaver dams near the farmhouse. By morning the only access road to Peck Farm would be flooded and we couldn't get out until we had axed-up the dam and destroyed the night-shift work of the redoubtable beavers, who wisely stayed out of sight during the daytime, though we thought we could hear them holding board meetings somewhere deep in their damworks. This axing was a fine and sure way of blitzing a morning hangover.

Afternoons we set up half a dozen chessboards and while listening to the Bobby Fischer *vs.* Boris Spassky world chess championship on the shortwave radio we'd try to keep a move ahead of the players. This feat was complicated by the circumstance that the moves were filtered in over the radio from Iceland and were given in Quebec French, and we had conflicting notions about the names of chesspieces in French and the radio static made the French moves additionally incomprehensible and so did the Jack Daniels Black Label.

We gathered eggs every morning — actually, that was my kid brother Marc's chore, which he found almost beyond his capacity, getting in the way of his poetry writing as it did. Thus the chickens suffered a crisis in morale, lost faith in the poetical soul of my kid brother and went on a slowdown, so that by the time we left Peck Farm the egg supply was a shameful trickle: one or two eggs per day from several hundred prize laying hens! Doctor Peck was stupefied, aghast, angry on his return and never spoke to any of us again. Father Hector Hoctor the Whisky Priest was there, "Chicken" Marengo was there, and poor dead Brad, and Marc, and me, and of course mad Madge just brooding on becoming a slut.

Right now she's married to an unemployed model airplane enthusiast. Or was that my second wife, Hortense? Shucks, that's right, it was Hortense who was with us. *(Hortense: Generic name for an ex-wife.)* She was pregnant then with my second kid — my eldest daughter, in fact. The past is a tricky time — I wonder why we think we need it.

No — come to think of it, my second wife was Corkie and

Hortense was the first one. I've got this all written down in a notebook somewhere, or I could look it up in the legal documents if I haven't thrown them all out, or if all the courthouses haven't burnt down. The only thing I can remember sharp and clear is my two little girls. But then it is years since I have seen them, much as I've tried.

That's what's wrong with reflection on one's own life, that's what makes it all break down — you start following a memory or a person in your past, and then you think of other people and then suddenly you are thinking of — your mind is naturally gravitating to — an unpleasant person or event when really you only want the good ones. Then the whole thing comes toppling down and the memoir itself, if you are writing one, goes haywire.

The silver earrings in Colorado . . .

They came from Cripple Creek. We finally *did* find the abandoned silver mines above the old wagon trail. Mandy and Gary and I did. Ricardo and Carbon Man stayed down in Cripple Creek loitering in front of the Old Fashioned Ice Cream Parlour.

Smoking Montecristo panatellas. Smoking the world's tastiest and most dangerous cigars. Talking deep philosophy. In full view of the police, while insolently looking over the gringo tourists, the beautiful Anglo women who were always streaming through the town in the summer. Carbon Man to be seen in sombrero; Ricardo in a cowboy hat looking like a real sinister Mexican type cowboy, lots of swagger, which is what he will be in another life, since that is what he is in this life.

Mandy was keen on seeing the old mines and I wanted to climb randomly in the hills and Gary wanted to inspect the cliffs from a more scientific perspective, so we climbed for nearly two thousand feet up above the town of Cripple Creek and could see its grid of streets laid out below us with sharp lines, and then every so often a cloud would pass over the town, darkening it, and we would be up where it was light and then the town would light up again when the cloud passed over and we would be where it was dark and would imagine Ricardo and Carbon Man down there in front of the Old Fashioned Ice Cream Parlour smoking their insolent Montecristos and casually surveying the beautiful Anglo women climbing in and out of the tourist buses.

We did find the old silver mines. Mandy had a good look, and Gary had a good look at the red soil up that high and started speculating about whole continents pushing up layers of rock from the very deepest levels and how they only came to the surface in Colorado where you can climb right up in the clouds above timberline to discover the way things are hundreds of fathoms *below* the surface of the Great Plains; the whole vast continent turned inside out and seen here as in X-ray vision.

And what about the silver earrings in Colorado?

In New York we had this outrageous stereo set (Heil AMP-1 towers for loudspeakers) when I was living with Carlotta on West 47th Street with the two Siamese cats, Jascha and Maya who moved like music, in clean clear Mozartean lines, through the studio. Cats like movable sculptures, plastic realisations of musical forms, the Mozartean impulse transposed into a feline dance in a New York studio with Carlotta's awe-inspiring body gliding naked or wearing only a pair of jeans, another purring realisation of silvery form.

Carlotta and her love for Mozart. Me and my love for Carlotta; and above the floor of the metropolis, twelve storeys up, the rain clouds passing down Seventh Avenue darkening the streets and then the streets brightening up as the clouds swept over.

Carlotta and her love of jewellery, of silver. . . . In Bennington, Vermont, we found an old silversmith who made us a pair of rings and in San Francisco we found their complement: a young craftsman at the Renaissance Fayre who designed us matching silver medallions, emblems of the Sun Energy on one side and the Earth Energy on the other.

So this very day I go randomly into a shop in Cripple Creek and I see them and buy them — silver earrings for Carlotta!

Then I go with Mandy and Gary up to the silver mines to explore the Earth Energy. Climbing above the city, the earrings in my pocket jingling away as we climb higher, even above the mines, towards the main peak, and we find when almost there — hard to believe! — a broad meadow filled with strange wildflowers (the whole scene becoming crammed with excessive idyllic romantic detail). And we're getting pretty tired so we stop and take off our backpacks and start gorging ourselves on salami on rye with dill pickles and a couple of apples. Gary has lugged up a sixpack of Coors beer which almost explodes when we open the first can. We pass it around and then another. And by the time we have finished them we are walking over the tops of the wildflowers seemingly without touching them and the sky is suddenly more beautiful, more absurdly blue — and Mandy takes off her shirt and her breasts start catching a lot of the Sun Energy up here.

Then Gary pulls her down and they roll over and over and they are kissing and then Mandy pulls me down too and rolls over on top of me and we are kissing, too.

The silver earrings are in my pocket — hey, they are getting crushed, and stabbing into my thigh!

We are all laughing — it must be the air over ten thousand feet. Mandy and Gary are getting ready to split up, they don't have much time for each other any more. It must be the altitude, rolling off of me she pulls Gary down again and they start wrestling and tickling each other until finally they are out of breath.

The difficulty is not in imagining exceptions to any rule, but in imagining the norm which is invisible. The everyday is invisible, while the exceptional is plainly seen. However, the unusual is quickly forgotten while the everyday, though invisible, is never truly forgotten.

So his trip to the North made a genuine thinker or reflective out of my Fijian friend Carbon Man, but I can't say how it all worked out.

None of my friends is an exception to the rule. And so all of them are for some reason memorable (to me). I have only forgotten exceptional friends, if I ever had any.

Lying together on our backs staring up at the absurd blue sky filled with Sun Energy and then falling asleep for a while until the mountain chill wakes us and we remember Ricardo and Carbon Man down there in the streets of Cripple Creek smoking Montecristos and maybe remembering us and looking up into the high hills.

SALAD RISING GREEN
TO THE MEMORY

Huge chords — Wagnerian chords — were pumping out of the loudspeakers.

He was listening to "Die Meistersinger" on compact disc while writing a poisonous little story in a postmodernist mode for one of the city of Doreen's better magazines. Somehow, Wagner helped him reach the right level of pretentiousness. On the television, sound turned down, was a one-day cricket match, Australia *vs* India. Cricket kept him closer to reality. One-day cricket kept him closer to vulgarity. So he could strike a balance.

Then there was the knock at the door.

Outside, there was blinding sunlight. A golden woman was standing there in running shorts and an inadequate halter-top. She was glistening after her run. This was the neighbour who had promised to drop in some day after her daily five kilometres.

"Wagner! Meistersinger! How did you know that is my favourite opera? You might succeed after all. In seducing me, I mean. I assume I read your transparent male mind correctly."

"Grotesque! So you think I want to... 'Seduce' is not even in my vocabulary! However... let's say that a friendly level of carnal knowledge is not out of the question in the distant future if you play your cards right.''

''You could be a very funny person — with lessons. But then you probably have been taking lessons for *quite a few* years.''

''So — uh — is Wagner all that brings you to my door?''

India was bowling and had just taken Alan Border's wicket for a duck. So it goes.

''I've decided to come for the sole purpose of showing you how to make a salad.''

''Que?'' His imitation of Manuel in ''Fawlty Towers''.

''I've come to show you how to make a salad. And I heard the Wagner. The whole neighbourhood can hear the Wagner.''

On the stereo, Wagner's contentious minstrels were preparing to show the gaping citizens of the town of Nuremberg just what it means to sing like a pro. But John-Paul hit the remote control and started the whole opera once again. A transparent stratagem.

She threw herself down on the bed, tired from her run. And began an ecstatic hum-along with the overture. She looked like the overture sounded — Wagnerian to the tips of her Adidas running shoes. And she did not seem to mind when he discreetly joined her in — or, more precisely, *on* — the sack. It *was* the best place in the house for listening to music.

''About that salad,'' she said.

''All I've got is lettuce in the fridge.''

They lay there for almost an hour, listening.

Then she turned to him: ''You got garlic?''

''I've always got that — I think.''

''You got salt?''

''Of course I got salt. That is, *maybe* I got salt.''

Then, tentatively, like Benjamin Franklin with his landlady, he ''attempted familiarities''. Also like Benjamin Franklin, he committed an *erratum*. So it goes.

The kitchen, he reflected, was by sheer neglect reduced to a postmodernist decorator's fantasy. She would see the innards of the kitchen glistening in the cruel afternoon sun. Electric cords running in all directions, looped over a complex array of servo-mechanisms, none of which had been cleaned in recent memory. (The electric pasta machine was the worst of the lot.) The rubbish bin was an overflow. The remains of a spontaneous lobster feast two days before, with Jan the barmaid, were beginning to draw attention to themselves. Could he stall her off? Keep her in or near the bed?

"Did I tell you my husband is a cop?"

"Husband? *Cop?*"

"Not really a cop. He's on the Star Force, the special branch."

"*Husband?*"

"Yeah, and a cop."

John-Paul fell silent for maybe the third time in his life.

"Relax, Tiger! We've separated on a trial basis."

John-Paul relaxed, a little.

"But he still comes over almost every night, and sort of keeps an eye on me. He's incredibly jealous."

John-Paul glanced at his watch in mock horror, as if he had suddenly remembered an appointment with his sharebroker or — hairdresser.

"Hey — isn't it getting late? We've sure been listening to a hell of a lot of Wagner. And — aw shucks! — I've still got a lot of work to do on this story for *Nemesis.*" On the TV he saw another Australian batsman get run out.

Trapped at the wrong end of the wicket! The Indians were jumping for joy. Brown skins, flashing white teeth.

"Forget it. I'm not leaving until I've shown you how to fend for yourself, salad-wise. You look like you live on junk food like *hamburgers* most of the time."

"Are you talking about my small but noticeable potbelly?"

She yawned as if she would soon be dropping off to sleep.

Food was an *obsession* since Hortense had left him. Every evening, almost, he went to a restaurant. He probably knew the dining-out scene better than most natives knew it.

Then, at a prompt from Wagner, she started up again, alert.

"Hey, *Seppo*, you got olive oil too?"

"Seppo?"

"Australian version of cockney rhyming slang. You are a Yank, sounds like septic tank. *Ergo* — 'Seppo'."

"Nice, a real sweet sound to it. But I got olive oil, for sure."

"My husband has killed three people — but that's in seven years on the force."

"I wonder how it feels — to kill."

"I wonder how it feels to eat a green salad without garlic."

"Your husband likes his food?" John-Paul was thinking it was time to get off the bed and brave the kitchen.

"Not really, it's just fuel to him. He has a high metabolism. He's incredibly fit, of course."

She changed her position on the bed so that the full stereo effect was not lost on her. John-Paul regarded it as a deliberately provocative writhing. But he was too often wrong about body language. He had been *very* wrong once, in '84 . . .

"Jeez, I crave it, really love it, the Wagner."

The ancients thought that eating was a sacred rite. To eat the wrong food at the wrong time was akin to blasphemy, and invited madness and death, or at least psoriasis, boils, dandruff. So the ancients were pretty careful about how they prepared their food. The moderns were a different story. Food just *happened* — at the end of a long but invisible production chain. Where do hamburgers come from? What do they *mean*? Questions of little interest to the fast-food junkie. The disappearance of God from everyday life was accompanied by the disappearance of cooking as a sacred activity. Then came the birth of civilisation and chronic gastritis.

The wife of the jealous killer-cop rolled over on her back as the last chords of Wagner washed over her well-tuned body. The delicate scent of her perspiration made John-Paul realise he was getting hungry. The ancients treated both eating and sex as sacred rites that were inextricably linked. And they threw in music as well.

The moderns had no opinion on this. The postmoderns were willing to reconsider.

"Hey, Seppo — I'm almost afraid to ask, but you got vinegar in there, likewise?"

"I'm almost afraid to look, but vinegar has got to be in there. *Malt* vinegar?"

"That's okay for the first time. For the first time you can get away with the malt, but later you'll need *wine* vinegar."

She gave John-Paul a chaste kissette and vaulted off the (king-sized) bed. He felt as if he had just lost a hand of canasta but was maybe winning the game.

What was canasta?

And what is to win?

The ancients believed that playing-cards and dice were sacred objects. The moderns discarded this belief, as it were. Cards were just like anything else, you could take them or leave them.

Now they were in the kitchen. John-Paul felt safer.

Taking the head of lettuce in one hand and a glistening knife in the other, the statuesque-blonde-jogger-and-Wagner-enthusiast-married-to-a-killer-cop slashed the lettuce neatly in half. Then she nicely severed the half-stem in two diagonal cuts. She selected the Thai-carved wooden salad bowl (John-Paul had never used it, except to feed Columbine, the stray cat, her daily ration of groats) and poured in a salad-spoonful of rock salt.

So the salad spoon was to be the basis of measurement?

"How do you peel a garlic, Seppo?"

"Carefully, with delicate shapely surgeon's fingers?"

"Quite utterly dismally wrong. You take a single clove and use the flat side of the knife and smash it *hard* with your huge hairy male seppo fist."

She was right — the naked garlic squirted out of its skin. Chop chop and the slick glandular garlic was in little bits. These were scraped into the bowl on top of the salad-spoonful of rock salt. Taking the wooden spoon she mashed the garlic into the rock salt, making a coarse paste. To this she added a single spoonful of Angelo Orsi deluxe brand olive oil, imported by John-Paul from California and never opened until now. The oil she blended into the garlic paste, thinning it out.

John-Paul went for the knife.

"Hey, you don't *cut up* the lettuce for this, Seppo. You *tear* it, leaf by leaf. This is a fully manual operation, right? And you got to make sure that each shred is tender lettuce and not stalky. Do you hear what I'm saying?"

"But, hold on — you forgot something. You forgot to add the vinegar!" John-Paul fairly lunged for the bottle of Woolworths malt vinegar. She was too fast for him and got between him and the bottle. This produced another Close Encounter of the Second-Best Kind. Smell. John-Paul could smell her hair and the garlic. And the salt even seemed to have a primitive smell of the Aegean about it. The cradle of civilisation. Salt-eating was the beginning of it all, right? Trade routes, etc. Commerce and all our subsequent troubles. The Rise and Fall of Empire. Settlement, eventually, of the city of Doreen itself. My God, what was this scented woman leading him *into?*

"Pay attention, Seppo! Not to worry about this vinegar just yet. We have the salt, the oil and the garlic in the bowl. We stirred it all together. Over that we have the lettuce. Now you just *fluff* the lettuce into the oil and garlic paste, until the paste is pretty well spread over all the little shreds."

This time he did as he was told. The afternoon was drawing on, the shadows outside were beginning to deepen. The Australia – India cricket-ground was in deeper shadow, since the match was in Sydney. Was he living on borrowed time now? The salad was now glistening with a dull sheen in the dark brown bowl. Deep green and dark brown in rich contrast.

By now he was beginning to trust her, sort of.

She sprinkled the vinegar — one salad-spoonful — evenly over the

22

lettuce. The oil seeped up from under, the vinegar rained down as from on high. This seemed meet and as it should be.

"You add vinegar only when you are ready to eat. We'll butter some of that full-corn bread and have it along with the salad. You've got a decent white wine in there, too. That will do to drink."

John-Paul opened the bottle with his old wooden corkscrew. (He couldn't find the pneumatic de-corker in its usual place.) This was one thing he *could* do. They took the bread and salad out to the verandah table, where he poured out two glasses. The wine would be decent, even a good one. He looked over at the woman who had so recently shared his bed, his music.

"Cheers."

She took one tiny sip.

"But you aren't touching your salad," he said.

"The salad is for you, Seppo. I have to go now. Thorstein will be expecting me — and I don't want him to start *looking* for me, if you follow my meaning. That always causes trouble, especially if his mates are along."

The woman who could make a salad like that just up and walked briskly out of his door, not looking back.

The cricket in Sydney was indefinitely halted by unseasonable hailstones. The TV was showing clips of past matches between the two sides. John-Paul put on the Overture to "Die Meistersinger", then collapsed onto his bed and began listening to the whole opera for the third time that day. Thus establishing some kind of a world record that never got written into the books.

That's all that happened.

Trust me, Thorstein!

Time and again, for many years after, John-Paul made that salad for himself and sometimes for others, never varying the ingredients or the procedure. It became almost the sole constant in his life, a ritual ordering. Sometimes he would turn on the Wagner before going to the kitchen.

Several women allowed themselves to be seduced with this salad, with the rich pretentious chords of Wagner as a contributing factor.

We must imagine now that some years have passed since the day described above. Thorstein is now chief of police in a smallish western metropolis. His wife, grown matronly, donates her time to Meals on Wheels. Confined now to a wheelchair — the result of a pantry accident (involving a newly purchased trash-compactor) — John-Paul can remember that original salad with bold clarity, as if it had been a still-life by Van Gogh. The woman of the salad remains in his memory, too, but now rather like a faded drawing by Willem de Kooning.

But the ageing writer, his mind glutted with the art and music of centuries, is still unable to summon up one image — that of Thorstein, his lifelong and endless rival.

It is not until the long night of his final struggle with the Angel of Death — with a little circle of mystified apothecaries, bloodletters and holy men in attendance — that the honoured writer John-Paul Maltravers can feel the lifting of the burden of the mystery.

And, expiring, cry out:

"Woman, you forgot one thing! *The freshly ground black pepper!*"

IN THE MAIZE

The two of us were working our way across the field. Our step-grandmother had bully-coaxed us into doing it. Gunny sacks slung, dragging through the loam, catching now and again on roots, stubble. We picked the sweet corn in the long, arrowshot rows, stooping down, reaching up high. The isobars were crowding one another on the weather map but the sky I remember as colouring-book blue.

That was in Iowa. Corn was everywhere.

And because there was the full corn, winter was ready to jab down from Canada's ice-fields and then we would be confined to tunnels of snow, more dead-straight rows. Cornstalks hissed, waved, muttered, and we were trying hard to bring full sacks back to Campbell.

Campbell was the farm lady who supplanted our real grandmother. Grandmother, an austere *memory* of a lady (handsome, white hair), lived in Denver with another old lady. She wrote to us three times a year — Easter, Christmas and on birthdays. What letters! The poetry of senile fancy, incomprehensible luxuriant caught-speech musings on her garden, pottings, mulchings, cuttings, creepers, the naughty cats' story cast in accents of fading birdsong, the gossamer never-recorded cadences of one old soul, bewildered in life's late garden heat.

But now we are concerned with Campbell — and shucking.

Picking it was not much fun, an overrated task, no amusement in it. But thereafter came the shucking...

It was nearing midcentury, when we were toiling up and down those corn rows. They were our family rows: opposite them the Olaffsen boys were doing their family rows too and beyond them you could see Michael Murphy (the sexfiend) all by himself as usual, but with a huge sack of corn bulging above him. The entire pre-pubertal male population of Strawberry Point was working those rows of Iowa corn. Quiet and businesslike, too, for behind each boy (a mile or so in the background) stood a threatening figure: a granny. A granny could wield a stick or a braided rope that was little less than a slavemaster's bullwhip when applied expertly to the burning body of a boy.

Byron (his name originally was spelt "Bjorn") was seven years old, a tow-head. I was nine but my hair was dark, curly and long. My mother and Campbell could not bear to see it cut. Dark curly hair was rare at Strawberry Point. Everybody was a tow-head, because almost everybody either came from Sweden or came from somebody who came from Sweden. The general principle and usage of the area was...to be Swedish. If you yelled out the name "Oscar" about fifty boys and a hundred grown men might start running in your direction.

There are probably two or three people in the world who have not ever seen corn shucked properly. In Iowa where the entire lifestyle was based on the behaviour of corn, it would be as needless to describe cornshucking as it would to print eating directions on fried chicken (our other great staple). It was something you just knew how to do. Later on, for some of us, maybe, sex came naturally, too. But many others probably needed to have directions printed on their wives on their wedding night. For there must have been some fellows who never had a kid like Michael Murphy around to tell them how things were done.

The theory of shucking corn sets forth the uninterrupted gesture. One twist of the wrist and the ear must be laid bare. It was Michael Murphy who showed us how to apply this principle of physical economy to other things...

Once the corn was picked from each family row the boys would line up with their sacks at the tailgate of the shucking truck, a slat-sided flatbed stacked with crates, each stencilled with a family name (a succession of alternating -bergs, and -sens): Knudsen, Olaffsen, Svenberg, Pedersen, Flachsenberg, Murphy.

Murphy?

Michael Murphy, sexfiend, lived right next door to us. Byron was the first to succumb to Michael Murphy's tuition. In later life Byron confessed to me about some of these episodes but the length to which practical instruction was carried remains obscure, now clothed in nightweeds forever.

The paths of life are always dividing, forking: left or right, boy or girl, same or different. The lives of my brother and me diverged in corn-row and briar patch, again and again, until in later life it did not seem as though we had ever been brothers at all. While Byron was learning about sex from a fiend, something different — call it an ideal — was being inserted into my brain. I was learning about love. The ideal of love came to me from comic books.

The comic book that most deranged me was called *Starry Eyes Comix,* which with admirable narrative gusto depicted the adventures of an impossibly beautiful girl-child. Her distinguishing feature was her starry bright-black eyes. The medium is the message: I fell in love with a cartoon.

Starry Eyes was cute the way Thumper and Bambi were cute. Big round eyes, long spiky lashes, a freckled button nose. And...

chubby cheeks. And . . . a little ballerina's tutu! It was a *red, white and blue* tutu. Like Wonder Woman, whom I fell for later, she wore sexy-patriotic dress.

Lying on my back in the old three-storey frame house, I would stare at the ceiling, watching the chandeliers sway as if they had suddenly changed places with me and were sprouting up from the floor. Lying there with *Starry Eyes Comix,* throbbing with love, I would dream up hideous new adventures, new slobbering malodorous malefactors to menace her — creatures whom a cartoonist would never dare to draw — to test again and again her virtue, her grace under pressure, her inexhaustible supply of pure energy. She was fuelled by a terrible innocence and purity. And . . . God could she sparkle!

It was painful to love Starry Eyes, like loving any celebrity. She could not be coaxed down . . . from the imaginary firmament, so to speak. I'd cry over and over:

"Please, Starry Eyes, come to see me, please please! Oh please, please, *please*!"

Please indeed.

My first wife, Donna, ex Mobile Alabama, would look as much like Starry Eyes as it was possible for any human being to do.

When the family rows of sweet corn were finally picked clean and the truck was loaded for the last time, the boys were carted off to the shucking. The women, girls and old men would be waiting at the shucking site. For in those days, the grown young men, and the fathers, were off at the war, overseas somewhere.

Our father was a bomber pilot, then, away training new pilots in Texas, a job only slightly more dangerous than his previous one of flying missions over Germany.

So the shuckings were manless. It was a time for everybody else to get together without the bother of having men around. Clean old country gentlemen (honorary females), for once useful, would build the bonfires.

Byron and I jumped off the truck, followed by Michael Murphy. A sexfiend should slither: Michael Murphy *slithered* off the truck, last of us all.

"Fetch thet gunny sack over here, puddin'," Campbell said, knowing that I was the only one who would follow her say-so. Byron was always a little slow in following orders, like in everything else. In the natural economy of the family there has to be one smart and fast boy and a slow and retarded one to set him off. Byron spent the rest of his life trying to outlive that role (BA, MA, PhD, Harvard).

The clean old men set up the huge steel pots and filled them from the pump next to the farmhouse. The farmhouse was owned by real country people — the Torgissens — who rented out strips of "acreage" for family planting. On the other side of the old stone house was more land for planting, too: the Strawberry Point graveyard. And beyond that, the church. The pots were for the cleanup, because after a few hours of shucking everybody is covered in corn-dust, like a mist.

It was not long before we loaded our first truck with bushels of shucked ears and the truck rumbled off down Merle Hay Road towards the communal silo. Merle Hay Road was named after the first Iowa boy careless enough to get himself killed in the war.

Meanwhile, in the farmhouse a mob of grannies was overseeing the fried chicken. Apricot pies were cooling on the back porch. Occasional forays by scent-crazed youths against these pies led to retaliatory search and destroy missions by the meanest and hardest of the granny-element.

The day wore on, and the truck came and went down Merle Hay Road for the last time. The pies cooled off, the chicken was brought out in tubs and exposed on the plank-and-trestle tables. The clean old men, after rescrubbing themselves in the pumpwater pots, were the first to eat. Somewhere, off in the larder, maybe, was the sacrosanct portion of dinner reserved for the grannies. They kept to themselves what was rumoured among us to be the choicest part: the giblets. Giblets! What are they ? They were accomplishments of the chicken we boys never got to taste. I have met grown men who still do not know what a giblet tastes like, nor what general region of the chicken it comes from.

At some time during the evening the grannies would steal away, perhaps in small groups, perhaps one by one, to savour the giblets in the pantry. Nobody ever saw a granny actually eat. The younger boys were of the opinion that a granny *never* ate! The only boy who claimed ever to have seen a granny *in flagrante* with a giblet was Michael Murphy — but then out of his area of expertise he was considered an unreliable narrator.

After the clean old men were done, the girls were marched forward to the fried-chicken table. They ate daintily and only picked at their food. They wanted to keep their dresses clean for the dance later on. And since they didn't want to get sticky fingers from the chicken, they polished off the tomato salads — which by a lucky chance were an abomination to the boys. Our many cousins were among the foremost in this little procession. The prettiest of them were two sisters, Sharon and Liz. Between them (at a mere twelve and fourteen years of age) they had cornered the market on good looks.

The boys stood round the perimeter waiting for a shot at the fried chicken. They would have to move forward cautiously: there were a *lot* of grannies here, quite a brutal turnout of them in force, since most of the mothers had gone off to work at the John Deere plant on the swingshift — where they made bullets, grenades and anti-personnel bombs.

By the time the boys licked the last of the chicken off their fingers, the sun was just about ready to drop down, as it does in the Midwest. There was to be a full harvest moon that evening. And the harvest moon meant there would be dancing after dark. Without a moon dancing would be considered lewd and lascivious conduct. That's how the Iowa people thought.

The Geezers, a five-piece string band of clean old men, began with the obligatory "Turkey in the Corn". My first partner was one

of the smaller grannies, a wizened little nun,
horse-chestnut, not more than eighty or ninety
dancing with — among — the gigantic-breaste
later I saw him sent spinning about by cousin L
sisters.

Then I was cast off by the granny and picked up
tried to waltz me around behind the shucking-moun   .ere was
danger of a kiss in this but, tired as I was from the picking, and the
shucking, and weighed down with fried chicken, I still managed to
manoeuvre Sharon out into the main ruckus of dancers, in company
with Liz and her new partner, who happened to be Michael Murphy.
They were doing some kind of wild jig to the waltz-time music.
(Though The Geezers preferred jigs and reels above all music, they
had been cautioned to concentrate on waltz-time, so as to preserve
public order.)

After a great deal of fancy dancing and general showing off,
Michael Murphy and Liz suddenly retired from the dancing-place,
soaking with sweat, and I didn't see them for a while after that.
Several hours later somebody tripped over Liz, dishevelled, sleeping
in a shucking-mound. Michael Murphy had slithered off somewhere,
maybe to an urgent appointment.

— Behind the shucking-mound together?

— There's no great harm in that, is there?

The harvest moon hung in the sky, like a firefly's answer to the
sun or a detective's golden flashlight. I thought I could actually see
its canals and hear its oceans, the waves sighing in the Sea of
Tranquillity, the pounding of the surf on the Murphean
Promontory...

— Whoa there. Send it past me one more time...*Murphean*
Promontory?

— It's on the map of the moon; go and look it up if you don't
believe me!

I met Elizabeth Murphy years later, in California, where by then
most Iowans had migrated, sunseeking, leaving the terrible blizzards

...ad. It was right after her divorce from Michael. We had a few piña coladas together in the Gander Lounge of the Rusty Duck, in Laguna Beach. A break-up from an ex-sexfiend can be a messy affair. One day Michael had disappeared with their two boys and for several months Liz heard nothing about them. Finally, on the leading-edge of a nervous breakdown, Liz hired a private eye who eventually found the boys — in Australia. That's a story in itself, Liz said. Now she was planning to marry again, a guy who got along terrifically with the boys. Sheldon needed a good woman in his life, after the troubles with Wanda.

As Liz got up to leave, I noticed that she was certainly a very attractive woman, that she had taken good care of her figure and was dressed expensively (a clinging dress in red, white and blue). But then every woman I knew in those days dressed expensively and went heavy on the make-up.

Driving back to the Laguna Plant of the Knudsen Corporation, I was churning management problems over and over in my mind but somehow they got all pushed aside by Liz's story about her kids (faithful to our Iowa past, she had named the elder son after me) and the later career of Michael Murphy.

Then I thought of the tragic life of my brother Byron, too — and somehow this all entwined with the immemorial scent of the sweet Iowa corn itself, and I began slipping back, right there in the smog of the Santa Ana Freeway, to a dream-world of golden maize, a world ruled over by those ancient corn-sprites called grannies.

And that is why, passing the Laguna Beach post office, I suddenly had a thought. I pulled up at the self-service window and bought a picture postcard (a pale slice of moon shown hanging over Balboa Island). Applying my pen to the picture side of the card, I carefully drew, superimposed upon the moonlit Pacific Ocean, a glistening field of Iowa cornstalks, row on row to infinity.

On the flip side I addressed the card to Campbell Knudsen, Ogallalla Rest Home, Keokuk, Iowa, and dropped it in the slot.

RAPPING WITH URIAH

Uriah drops in for a yarn; the high point of his day. Uriah works in the other division, Domestic Division, and is sometimes inquisitive about my North American contract, which of course I can't talk about, particularly as I myself know little about the situation and work blind most of the time. But Uriah wants his little chat.

Uriah's conversational gambit for the last few months has been his car battery. Should he get a new one? Should he wait this one out to the very end? It is an old battery, but he drives a high-performance machine. So this battery — an Alcoa, incidentally — has to be recharged every so often — indeed, some forty or fifty times in the last few months. He regaled me, on each of those occasions, with the full details: the Royal Automobile Association would jump-start him and then heartlessly recommend a new battery.

But now the RAA are no longer blissful about the jump-starts. Recently there have been instances of refusal, and counter-stratagems have had to be used (ringing the RAA from a friend's house, hiding behind the lounge-room curtains while the friend passed off the car as his own, etc.).

So now, more than ever before, Uriah wants to open discussion about *whether he should buy a new battery*. And if it must come to pass, what kind should he buy, as he does not want to get "ripped off". Uriah is an affluent man and for perhaps that very reason is extremely careful about his money. Which is piling up like cowflop in the bank. Truth to tell, he's a flaming miser.

I tell him sure there are several good brands of batteries and as many that ought to be avoided, as well as several brands I know nothing about. The Goldmark IV is high-priced but delivers power over long periods and in most climates but in this mild climate with only the rainy and the dry seasons perhaps the investment in the Goldmark IV might not be warranted. Cell breakdown is minimal in the Tigress PC-3 distributed by Auto-Technics, Inc., and it has an admirable record of reliability. Maybe a shade better is the Climax Sport Three if you are only interested in mild-climate function, but with a high-performance engine. It's a bit dearer again, however, and might not be worth the extra money. Everything hangs on the question of how many starts a day you are interested in. If you only want four to six starts a day then a better deal (with an impressive record of cell stability) is the Velocity Ranger in the middle price bracket, but my own experience has been somewhat disappointing up above that dreamy, almost mythic plateau of six starts a day, especially if I am romancing Fiona and don't do much driving between starts but need many quick, sudden ones. Bruno, her husband, is a jealous man.

Uriah is not sure he's ready for a new battery but will keep me posted and look into the matter a bit more, seek some more advice from a number of other (the implication is, "more reliable") colleagues, talk to his mechanics and their mates next time he drops in at the garage.

Misers, as has been well documented, pay excessive attention to money. But they are legendarily more interested in saving money than in earning it. When I bought my house from Uriah he was so concerned with closing the deal before the monthly mortgage payment fell due that he sold me the place for a song — well below a fair market value.

Not a colourful anecdote, admittedly, when you think of the many good miser jokes making the rounds. But I write to inform, not to titillate.

It was a cold and intermittently rainy day when next I heard from Uriah on the subject of the battery.

What ho! What was the news, I asked, what were the latest developments?

He remained silent for some time, chewing on his pipe-stem, an old ''niggerhead'' meerschaum his father had left lying around one day and had never been able to locate since.

He preserved silence — knowing that the right time would come to break it all to me. We were having lunch together at the Club. Uriah had forgotten to buy his round of beer. The windows were steamed over, and, outside, tiny sparrows in search of a final warmth were beating their tiring wings against the glass. Ironically, it was hot and steamy in the Club. Over in a far corner several gentlemen were conducting a cabernet sauvignon wine-tasting. Their roars and bibulous guffaws could be heard clear across the room. They were no respecters of the peace.

Uriah hung fire until he believed he had chosen his time. His beer glass was empty.

''I have finally decided to buy a battery,'' he said.

''Oh?''

''I have been in contact with a certain gentleman, an agent.''

''Yes? And?''

''In short I shall be going ahead.''

''Going ahead? When?''

His eyes were alert, full of the sense of the adventure.

''At the first of the month or thereabouts.''

''Let me get this straight. At the first of the month you will be *purchasing a particular battery* for your car?''

I had put it too strongly. He recoiled sharply.

"Not — not exactly *purchasing*. At least...not in the first instance. I shall be trying it out for a short time — on approval. But you might say, the upshot is, that by the next time we meet I shall probably have purchased myself a battery. Does that, uh, *surprise* you?

"It's just that — it seems so...sudden."

"And...Ulrich, if you will kindly hear me out."

"Yes, Uriah?"

There is a decorous pause while I pay the girl for another round of beers. One does not exchange confidences in front of serving people.

"I trust you will not spread this around. Bruit it about to the first passerby you see."

He fixed me with his glare.

I produced an expression I thought conveyed quizzical innocence, or, perhaps, innocent quizzicality.

"Like you did about the *vacuum cleaner*."

"The...?"

"The vacuum cleaner — back in 'seventy-nine."

I knew then, in that instant, that our Past is something at once obdurate and luminous, and that it is entirely at the mercy of the people we choose to know.

I bowed my head and lowered my eyes.

"Trust me," I said.

DREAMFEEDINGS

When his wife left him to return to England he found himself at loose ends. She had said nothing about coming back. Things hadn't been going well for them. They had no children. All they had between them was the big half-furnished house and the animals. The fiction was that they were her animals, and so he normally took no responsibility for their care. Then, when she suddenly left him, he discovered he had a menagerie on his hands. Two dogs, three cats and an operatic canary.

They refused to eat the food he set out, so he had to experiment. (What had his wife been feeding them? He had never bothered to notice.) He was persistent, buying them the most expensive, exotic morsels he could find in the shops — poached eel, smoked salmon — in the hope they would start eating again. Soon, grudgingly, a few of them began to come over to the new regimen. He was so pleased when they would consent to eat what he brought them. Eventually even Churchill — the surliest cat — capitulated and all was well; a peaceable kingdom re-established.

The canary — named Onan because of his tendency to scatter his seed — came finally to accept his double ration of imported Royal Songbird Mix. And began to sing like there was no tomorrow.

But one day Armstrong got a terse, chilly letter from his wife. On half a page of hotel stationery, the lower edge a jagged rip. She had decided to live on a trial basis with an old boyfriend in Scotland. She would let him know how it all worked out.

And how were the animals doing?

That night the first of a series of dreams began. In these dreams, instead of living in the Australian suburban flatlands, he found himself in a high-rise apartment in a strange city. He decided it must be New York, the city he had lived in before coming to Australia. The building seemed still to be under construction, though crawling with occupants, mostly young freaked-out types who gave all-day, all-night parties. The parties were held among the girders of the building, which, as in some postmodernist fantasy, were exposed. You could look down from where you perched and see a twenty-storey drop to the streets below. The freaks did not seem to notice this, as they smoked dope and reeled from one end of their partly completed flat to the other. As there were no walls, just a floor with lots of gaps in it, cyclonic winds whistled through. They all sat in circles and talked about films they liked. Armstrong, a somewhat older man, would come to their door and, since he was their next-door neighbour, they would grudgingly let him join them. There were several women in this group and Armstrong found himself seated next to one or two of them. He rarely joined in the conversation, which was about things he had no knowledge of.

In his own apartment next door he discovered two kittens and a scruffy black pup of indeterminate breed. When it was feeding time the kittens would make a death-defying leap from an outside girder to the window ledge. Each time they almost did not make it to the sill, but they always did. Armstrong doted on them but was terribly afraid they would not — one day — make it to the ledge and would fall, claws scrabbling, to the street twenty floors below. He would feed them, lock the apartment (which, oddly enough, said "Private

Detective Agency'' on the door) and go around to his neighbours' and sit in that circle, always calculating how he could get closer to the girl he fancied most. She wore jeans and a loose checked shirt (no bra, obviously) and never seemed to comb her hair. She paid no attention to him whatsoever.

Then Armstrong would awaken. The day-cats would be up on his bed wailing for their tuna in brine. The real dogs would be licking his face, eager for their baked Alaska.

Another day in the real world.

Invariably, there was an empty scotch bottle beside his bed. The longer his wife was away the cheaper the brand of scotch became. Soon there would be no cheaper scotch and he would have to find something else to put him to sleep. He had to go to sleep, he knew, because he had to feed the pets in his dream. He was afraid that if he missed a night they would go hungry. If he did not knock himself out with booze he would not sleep at all. And the dream animals were waiting for him. If he were not there to receive them they might one day miss that ledge and take the long fall to the street.

So in his waking life he was feeding one set of animals and in his sleeping life the others would appear at the window sill of the Private Detective Agency, mewling for their meals, stroking him when fed. Once in a while a client would appear at the agency door, which was of stippled semi-transparent glass. He could see their shadows as they approached. They wore hats, invariably, with wide brims and had grey suits. A police detective once appeared and asked him to keep an eye on the kids next door. Let him know what they were up to.

He continued to go to the gatherings next door. An exotic array of people — all of them quite young — would be coming and going. A boy in a yellow T-shirt with ragged sleeves would perch on a girder and hang out over the street. This would make some of the girls laugh. Armstrong still sat quietly next to the girl in the checked shirt, agreeing with everything she said but totally ignored by her.

But then things started to get hectic in the daytime. Armstrong's boss, as if sensing how tough it was with his wife gone, kept on driving him, harder, with more and more assignments, seemingly impossible demands. He was given new contracts to handle, and the wording on the agreements seemed more and more confusing to him. And yet the boss would not let up. He sensed a weak spot and, never having liked Armstrong very much, started putting on the pressure. Armstrong found himself taking a lot of work home at night and staying up long hours poring over the contracts, which might as well have been written in Sanskrit so far as he was concerned. Then he would have to compose detailed commentaries and offer full suggestions as to how the assembly-process should be implemented. For over a week he only got an hour or two of sleep per night, and yet the boss was still not content and insisted that the plans be thought through again — by Monday, or Friday, or Thursday.

Armstrong's wife was now sending only postcards — mostly of picturesque castles in Scotland. Rory was taking her on a grand tour of the land of his ancestors.

And . . . and how were the animals?

Once, in the middle of the night, while Armstrong was slaving over some assembly-line diagrams, the phone rang. It was his wife, sounding as far away as the dark side of the moon. She wanted to know if he was taking good care of the animals. And she wanted a word with the labrador, who yelped loudly into the mouthpiece when he heard her voice. Then she rang off without further conversation with Armstrong. He woke at his desk the next morning after a dreamless sleep.

The work was becoming impossible. Armstrong tried calling in sick but that only made the boss come to his house, a whole portfolio of papers in hand, and tell him there was another deadline on the assembly contracts. He could hear the purr of the boss's BMW, mingled with the purr of Mrs Craddock, senior cat of the premises, who was insisting on her time on Armstrong's lap.

Armstrong had not shaved for several days. His eyes were pinched and bloodshot, stabbed by the daylight. It was all he could do to crawl to the corner deli to fetch the tuna in brine and the poached rabbit fillets for the animals. As for himself — he was not eating. He forgot to eat. He chewed an occasional cabana sausage or ate a bag of potato chips. And sipped the cheap scotch.

Then one evening, to his horror, Armstrong remembered that he had forgotten to feed the other animals, the two kittens and the puppy at the Private Detective Agency. How long had it been — a week, two weeks? He really could not remember. He had been so loaded down with work and worry. He had forgotten them!

The way to the dream was through the scotch bottle. Armstrong opened a new bottle, pushing aside all the accumulated papers on his desk, and poured himself a tumbler full of scotch. His hands were shaking and it took both of them to convey the liquid to his mouth. He was terribly worried that, in the land of the dream, he could never thread his way back to the place he wanted, to his point of responsibility. When the bottle was about half empty, the doorbell rang. He stumbled out of his study, dragging the typewriter to the floor behind him.

The boss was standing there in a grey suit with a neat, conservative striped tie. He looked at Armstrong — aghast. He held a portfolio of papers in his hand (neatly manicured nails!) which he did not, as was his usual practice, thrust at Armstrong. He scrutinised Armstrong for a moment — there was almost a glint of compassion in his eyes — and then turned quickly on his heel and left. A well-tuned BMW purred away into the night.

Armstrong, fully clothed in what was now a somewhat foul-smelling warm-up suit, crawled into his bed. It was a chilly winter's night. The animals were soporific in front of the fire in one promiscuous heap. At any rate, *they* had been well fed!

Then, in the labyrinth of the dream, Armstrong sought the unfinished building with the Private Detective Agency. The streets of the city were deceptive, convoluted, but he allowed instinct to guide him. Finally he thought he had found the building and, by dint of sheer willpower, he dreamt himself up to the upper storey. Sure enough, there was the glass door with the words Private Detective Agency embossed on the stippled glass. He fumbled with the key but it did not seem to fit. Next door he could hear a party in full blast. A door opened behind him and somebody called his name. It was the girl in the checked shirt. "Where have you *been* lately, Armstrong?" she asked with a smile. The top two buttons of her shirt were undone. She was obviously still not an advocate of the bra. She led Armstrong by the hand into her apartment, which was still exposed to the howling winds above the city, and Armstrong negotiated a tricky passage across the floor-beams, through which he could see the street so far below. Everybody in the room welcomed him as if he were a long-lost friend. They passed a glowing pipe around to him and he took a few long pulls on it. The girl was leaning against him, running her hand up and down his back.

It was then that he thought of his animals.

He jumped up and ran for the doorway. But it seemed hours before he could get there. Once gaining the passageway, he found his own door: Private Detective Agency. This time the key turned miraculously in the lock, and Armstrong entered.

What he saw was not pretty. The kittens were now only two shrivelled little balls of fluff. The puppy, almost ludicrously, was lying on its back, in its final death throes, four paws twitching in the air. The poor mutt! In the quivering of those tiny paws, all of Armstrong's dream seemed to roll up and carom away from him.

Predictably, as in so many dreams of the human race, he was falling, falling from that tremendous height. And then he hit bottom, the cruel pavements of that strange city.

No — he landed (as we dreamers do) in his own bed. And somebody was there, too, somebody rubbing his back, up and down his back, the way he liked to be touched.

And speaking to him.

"Three cheers! You actually took good care of my little monsters! I thought they would go to rack and ruin, with *you* looking after them. That's why I decided to come back — to *save* my babies.''

Her coat was on and she bore with her all the chill of the morning. Armstrong looked at his wife.

''Don't ask about Rory,'' she said. ''Don't even mention that name in my presence. God! He was just like you — a first-class bastard.''

MAYBE HE SHOULD SELL
TO THE ITALIAN

To Maxie Fogel, general magazine merchant in our city of Doreen, the world is no longer the fine sort of place we all think it is. You might well ask why.

"Maybe I ought to sell to the Italian," Maxie Fogel is thinking.

Ever since the opening of the Panorama Superserve right down the street his business had begun to go on the skids. His main customers had been presentable elderly men who had been coming to the shop for as many as ten years to buy magazines filled with pictures of naked girls no older than their grand-daughters. He could see them now, slinking past on their way to the Panorama Superserve, where the selection was better and the prices were lower.

"I don't like the story of my so-called life," Fogel says bluntly to himself.

Sleep has been eluding him lately. For many years sleep has been an angel of whims, a devouring angel, never his deliverer. And yet he had invoked her with soft and then urgent breath, rising to a hymn of supplication in the hour before many a blinding dawn.

Sure, and then Angel-Sleep would come — at six in the morning, which was precisely the moment the alarm would go off. In the years gone past, with Wanda, this meant that Fogel would have to be up sweeping the floor of the liquor store they lived over.

That was on Centennial Boulevard in Los Angeles.

Wanda had not been overly comforting in those predawn anguishments. Which was partly Fogel's fault. A talkative man, Fogel was fond of constructing theories of sleeplessness. Composing those theories kept his mind and tongue agitated through the hours of tossing and turning. But Wanda — dead now these last ten years — was not a talkative woman even while she was alive. Talk, for Wanda, was a dangerous luxury. For Wanda loose talk could sink ships.

She never said a word about her own troubles, which Fogel knew in his heart to have been immense. Her life one long ache. Her son was dead at eighteen. The boy had been the product (or rather the *quotient*) of a first marriage that had been supercharged with calamities. Wanda loved a man, the bum Kopecks. Everybody warned her against having him. It is given to every woman to meet such a bum once in her life. And it is given to most of them to have the good sense to walk away from him.

So poor Wanda threw herself away on the bum Kopecks, who in all his life had never known a week of — you name it — sobriety, chastity, decency...equanimity.

Rudy, the son, grew up bad, too. He was a real nasty piece of work. The kid became known in the neighbourhood as Bloody Rudy (for reasons Wanda never enquired into). Most bad kids are bad because they fall into bad company, start running around with the wrong sort from the other side of the tracks. This could not be said of Rudy: like his old man, *he* was the bad company other kids fell into on their way to the San Quentin gas chamber. Sure enough, true to his promise, at the age of eighteen Bloody Rudy was shot dead by a security cop — during a midnight caper at a construction site. Wanda, watching the evening news roundup of that day's disasters in LA, saw her own son's body being dumped not in kindly fashion into a police ambulance. The next morning she was waiting at the City Morgue to identify Rudy's remains. She said little at the time, only "yes".

Nowadays, Fogel, who must not be regarded as an old man, has no wife. He does have his canary Pavarotti.

There had been a robbery, during which Wanda was gunned down by a drug-crazed *pachuco*.

Maxie Fogel at that particular time, let me say it to his shame, was cowering in the toilet at the back of the shop.

The widower, who was not getting any younger, decided to emigrate to Doreen, in Australia. A friend who had made some money selling fibreglass swimming pools decided to start a journal of the arts and industry. Fogel was known among his friends as something of a cultured man. He wrote poetry which his friends would carry around in their wallets out of sheer admiration. The LA streets were not thick with poets. Fogel's scribblings put him shoulders above his friends. Many a street punk carried a Maxie Fogel poem wadded up with his bankroll, and he might whip it out to read to some girl he was trying to shake down.

Fogel had published in trade journals like the *Fiberglass Age, Mortuary Horizons* and *Die and Moulding Market Review*. Then he struck poetical paydirt: *Arizona Highways* accepted the poem "Earth Deity", which immediately soared to the top of the hit parade among the boys who worshipped the writings of Maxie Fogel.

So it was right he should answer the call to Australia. He was preceded by a series of articles — short prose poems, really — in *Australian Fibreglass Era*, celebrating the wedding of man-made materials with plants and stones in backyard pool applications. It was on the strength of this sequence — called "Synthetic Solar Breeze" — that the Australian immigration officer admitted M. Fogel to Australia as a Permanent Resident. Permanent Residents were obliged to have skills in short supply in Australia. Fogel was admitted as a "writer/publicist".

Maxie Fogel is thinking, "Maybe I should sell to the Italian." The Italian does not exist except within Fogel's brain.

His brain he would himself describe as a nice place to visit (but who would want to live there — right?).

Fogel's brain is as convoluted as a map of Los Angeles. Which is maybe why the neat, foursquare streets of our city of Doreen disoriented him from the first: he was walking (and driving, and thinking) in gigantic loops, while everybody else was taking the corners square. The magazine failed. The wedding of business and poetry was never consummated.

That was ten years ago. In the present, Fogel is saying to himself, ''Maybe I should sell to the Italian.''

Somebody up there must have changed his mind about Maxie, for today, just when business has reached its absolute nadir, the Italian actually arrives. This is much to the astonishment of Maxie, who believes that no wishes emanating from any brain of his own could ever come true.

Sure, the Italian arrives, but the twist is, the Italian is a girl about eighteen years old or so.

Her eyes are rather remarkable. Looking into them is like scanning a road map of Los Angeles. Convolutions in brown, tinged with asphalt-grey. But be warned, Maxie, they are the eyes of an angel of insomnia! Or at least the eyes of a waif. Maxie savours that antique descriptor for a moment. Fogel meets waif. She's looking for a magazine on bird care, would you believe? But also she succeeds in drawing Fogel into conversation about how's business. The proprietor finds himself poor-mouthing his own business. But the girl seems to listen only to the *good* things he says about life as a small business proprietor.

The blessings of running the shop are soon told: you don't have to spend a lot of time getting along with the customers, as at present there aren't that many. But there are enough of them, you understand, to keep things going — at least for now. The same could not be said of next week perhaps. But fortunately life is short. And taxes are in this case low.

She buys a copy of *Australian Avian Age* and vanishes.

Two weeks later the Italian returns to the shop, looking for a copy of *Modern Australian Budgie*. She is decked out in the same threadbare weeds as before but there is a new kind of a glow to her, if you know what I mean. I mean the Los Angeles eyes have abated, the map has been folded up, or gone out of print and it's been replaced with something else — something not as disturbing and with more of a punch to it. But do I need to elaborate on the ways a certain kind of girl can affect a middle-aged man? Maybe youth is the sauce, as Mother Fogel used to say.

Maxie knows it's two weeks later because he has been thinking about this girl. A lot... But not daring to really expect to see her again. And now she asks for *Modern Australian Budgie*? There is no such magazine of course.

But once again they have a little conversation. Of course, business is no better than before, Maxie has to report. But he is expecting things to get better. Maybe — if spring comes early this year.

Then, to make a long story short, the girl comes out with it: she lays her life story on poor Maxie (known to be a good listener). Sigmund Freud would say she has obviously spent her life looking for a father-figure type. Her real father was a very wealthy man who owned a construction company. But the rich man and his daughter never saw eye to eye. He disapproved of everything: her smoking, her boyfriends, her hippie lifestyle, even Proud Beauregard (her pet budgie). One day he beat her up, threw her out of the very house she had grown up in. Proud Beauregard fled to the nearest treetop where he was welcomed — and instantaneously executed — by a transient rosella. The girl lived around for a few years, wherever somebody would take her in, getting into drugs a little, and — uh, yeah — a little prostitution...

She still kept track of her father, but from a discreet distance. She would send him a Valentine once a year, with her own verses written on them.

You see, she's a lover of poetry. It's got its fingers into her soul. Somehow she had learned on the street that Maxie Fogel — a man in whom she sensed a past suffering and a well-developed soul — had been a poet. So she had gone to the Doreen Public Library and had found the "Synthetic Solar Breeze" poems. She was duly impressed. Then one day in a back issue of *Arizona Highways* she had found a treasure, the poem "Earth Deity". This poem had blown her away, reduced her to a puddle of tears.

Leaving the library she rang her father to beg his forgiveness (for the way *he* had treated *her*? Maxie thought). Her father told her that as a matter of fact he was dying of cancer, had only a few weeks to live. He asked her if she wanted anything to remember him by.

She told her father she wanted to buy a magazine shop.

She went home to care for him in his last days. In the few weeks they enjoyed together they became closer than ever before. It was like going back to the days when she was his little girl.

Then he had died, only a few days ago.

So she is here to make Maxie Fogel an offer he can't refuse.

Maxie doesn't exactly catch the amount she names — it's more than enough. Enough to retire with and maybe to publish a small magazine of his own. Maybe the spousal verse of the mind of man and synthetic materials will some day still be sung. Maxie at this point in time is thinking of lots of things — Wanda! Rudy! — but also the Italian.

Whose name he doesn't yet know.

That night, Maxie gives Pavarotti a double ration of highest quality Palermo brand imported birdseed. The Italian is of course still on his mind. In fact bits of opera, *The Magic Flute* (but not an Italian opera, mind you!) flitter through his brain, alighting here and there. Among them is Papageno's happy little ditty, the one song Mozart called for on his deathbed, which at this moment has flown from Mozart's brain to Maxie's. And why not? It is the *birdcatcher's* song. Maxie whistles it, and Pavarotti warbles along, too.

As if that were not enough, the lonely Jewish merchant opens a can of Cal-Mex imported tamales for his dinner (wishing it were lasagna!). Such is the romance lurking in our souls, particularly in the souls of poets. Instead of watching the television, Maxie takes out a few yellowed drafts of poems. He looks up at the wall plaque and remembers he has not actually read his poem "Earth Deity" since arriving in Doreen. It's been mounted on the wall all that time — ten years. His memory takes him on a free first-class trip back to the Old Country, Los Angeles. He opens a can of beer, wishing it were chianti. The alcohol wafts into Maxie Fogel's wayward brain and his thoughts become grander. Maybe... maybe he's a man of parts, after all. Maybe his poetry days aren't behind him forever.

Sitting down to his typewriter he composes something — a poem perhaps — for the girl. Of which I offer you a fragment (from the first draft):

To the Italian Girl of Payneham Road

I remember your unspoken name like it was my daughter's
I remember your eyes like twin maps of a faraway city
I remember my mother's promise I would meet you
I remember the squares of this city where I would eat apples,
    sharing my lunch only with the smaller birds, never the gulls
I remember the poetry that lived once in my thoughts and the
    name I gave it
I remember when takings were low you spoke to me of who I
    was
I remember...

This is an example of the refreshment of Maxie Fogel's soul by the spirit of poetry, ever awakening at the approach of love.

I know, I know — Mozart again! The books, the movies, the rock opera, the T-shirts, all that Mozart hype. But I had made some discoveries, had found out some very hot stuff on Mozart...

I had guarded Mozart's secret for many years, until one day I revealed all to Margot. I suppose I did so because I knew she did not have long to live and I wanted to share something with her at the end. But Margot urged me, as a favour to her, to write some of it down — not all by any means, for that would be too dangerous. For it had geopolitical implications, involving the balance of power between Eastern and Western bloc nations.

So it was agreed I would write one of the world's missing books, *The Childhood and Death of W. A. Mozart*. All Margot's wealth and influence would be placed at my disposal. I would withdraw to the Southern Hemisphere, to the city of Doreen-by-the-Sea, so as to gain the proper distance. There, beneath the crazed pattern of the southern stars I would meditate and write. I would be supplied with a high-performance automobile, a yurt on Amethyst Island, a small villa in the northern suburbs of Doreen, and an office in the city centre twelve storeys above the Boulevard Raspail, Boulevard of Authors, which, incidentally, is graced with an equestrian statue of

General Leopold Mozart, author of the boy-genius. That statue is why we chose Doreen. It suggested a pattern.

The day of my arrival I saw the Queen of Doreen herself, pacing with great dignity down the Terrace Raspail with its statues so objectionable to Ernest Hemingway ("Always of *dead* writers!"), and next to her the diminutive Consort. There was no attempt on her life that day.

I arrived the day before the rain-and-neurosis season was due to begin. The next day it rained like hell and a gunman ran amok on the Terrace. I was at the time stowing my gear in my office: suddenly I heard gunshots close at hand. I took the lift to the ground level to get a good look at what was going on.

The gunman staggered out of the Central Armoury seemingly drunk, dragging two shotguns at each side in pathetic approximation of the "trail arms" position. And above him — I could see and he could not — there was the public sharpshooter in the Carpark Tower, levelling an Armalite rifle. Two panicked policemen ran past me, squealing a warning. They flattened themselves in the archway of St Cecilia's church. In the midst of this ruckus — which reminded me of my beloved New York City — I heard the burp of the canister — and got hit with a strong whiff of it — the tear gas. The sharpshooter outleant precipitously from an aperture in the Tower.

Tear Gas produces a universal and *involuntary* reaction. It is one of the great levellers. We all think we want to buy into whatever is universal and involuntary. Tear Gas — a modern absolute, a transcendental ideal, an elective affinity? Every writer, composer, artist, wants to write, compose, draw — *in the manner of Tear Gas.*

I tried, like the others, tears in my eyes, to get a good look at the new corpse in the city of Doreen. But they drew the ambulance curtains quickly, as if ashamed of their madman.

I spent the weekends in my yurt, taking the Amethyst Island ferry over for breakfast at Aunt Annie's Cafe and pacing with an isolato's dignity along the boardwalk of Doreen. The girls on roller skates, the unicycles propelled by juvenile delinquents. I began writing, partly in my head, the book on Mozart. There was also a manila folder of notes — my own handwriting frightening me a little, filling every visible scrap of paper. The Magic Flute, Papageno the Birdcatcher, Mozart on his deathbed calling for Papageno's merry birdcatching song. If this will be it, the end, then why not die happy, eh?

Shall I never return and play that song for you, Margot?

Mozart on the day of his death is looking at himself in the mirror. Maybe having forgotten what he looks like. Mozart's desk is cluttered with scraps of music paper filled up on both sides. He is a little frightened of his own handwriting now he's going to die of influenza and neglect. The mirror mordantly staring, challenging, reassuring:

Turn again, Mozart! Greatness will be yours!

The bloodletting basin imaged in the corner of his yellow eye. Mozart's curvilinear perspective in the glass is crammed with excessive detail.

Mozart: recollecting his dream of the Tower of Rats, the Paradise of Flies, the Kingdom of Maggots. But then he thinks of the power of joy and — *the song of Papageno!*

Books about Mozart, how many are being written in the silent towers of Doreen? The statue of Colonel Leopold Mozart overlooking the city, pointing into the sky, the tear-gas sky of Doreen.

I look into the cracked mirror, see in the corner of my scholar's eye page one of the manuscript of the book on Mozart, my book on Mozart.

Mozart, like Bach, drank too much coffee.

I drink too much coffee.

Some weeks later, the Doreen weather, never very settled, was climbing to an unseasonable high. I was walking back to my office for another session on the Mozart book — my challenge, my responsibility, perhaps my albatross.

Turning the corner onto the Boulevard Raspail, the most depressing street in the world, I get a nasty surprise. I nearly collide with a woman as she hobbles out of the corner wineshop. That woman happens to be my ex-wife, Maisie!

What the hell is she doing here, in the Southern Hemisphere?

Maisie says her day has been rotten enough already without having to meet me. Her second husband Boris has been hassling her, pumping her for information about my doings and undoings. Is it true that I am here to do a book on Mozart? What gives? And why all the secrecy about it?

Maisie is still the same, rattling on, unable to keep quiet about anything. She's talking so loud that passersby can hear the whole exchange.

I can't quite forget that Boris once swore he'd "get" me. And he is a tough customer: ex-Green Beret, and ex-CIA operative who used to hang out in the dirty tricks department. He had a special flair for interrogation and was never so happy as when he was toppling handcuffed suspects out of helicopters.

So — I ask — uh, where *is* Boris?

But for once Maisie won't blab. In fact, as if disgusted by my own uncooperativeness, she wheels about and vanishes around a corner. Great! Just great! Nice to know these folks are in town!

If they ever find out what I'm onto about Mozart...

Later, on my way to the Maid and Magpie for a quiet drink with the barmaid, I run into Maisie again lurching out of the chemist shop.

"My period's starting," she shouts, for the benefit of passersby, as if it were my fault.

MOZART NOTES

The child Mozart's bedroom faced west. Jack Frost would fine-etch the window pane during the winter nights and you could trace that magical handiwork with talented fingertip in the morning. In the rosy glow of morning, the dawning-time of genius.

The charmed casement opened to the west, opened to America. See a city map of Salzburg. He would have a terrific view of the sunset, but as for the dawn...

Mozart's bedroom had an old-fashioned closet or wardrobe where he fitted out a little "Papageno nest" and set up housekeeping with Marie-Antoinette, the girl next door — a somewhat older, more experienced girl, a bit cynical about boys. Mozart and Marie-Antoinette snuggled up naked in this darkened stifling wardrobe closet because they were playing prince and princess and they had never heard of a prince or princess being described as fully clothed.

Mozart was experiencing in a subtle fashion the first stirrings of what Sigmund Freud would later call polymorphous perversity.

Then there is the Oedipus Complex: Wolfie on the day of his death remembered the hallway where he first saw, clothed in shadow, a certain returning soldier: his father, the Colonel, home from the Hundred Years' War. The soldier standing tall and dark beneath the hanging burberry tallow candles.

This soldier would now sleep in Mrs Mozart's room down the hall. And Wolfie would not be allowed to creep into his mother's warm bed in the middle of the night. Not now that Colonel Leopold Mozart was in there.

Once upon a time Wolfie had a dream and he started creatively sleepwalking. He walked down the tallow-candled hallway in the cold winter night and entered the bedchamber where his mother and the tall dark soldier were heavily sleeping off the effects of the Hundred Years' War.

Walking in his sleep the little Mozart missed the left turn to the en suite water closet and entered his mother's wardrobe, thinking perhaps it was his own little Papageno nest. The child Mozart felt a stirring, his periwinkle throbbing in the night air as he relieved himself copiously over his mother's delicate silk and fur garments. And Freud would not be born for over a hundred years!

Mrs Mozart then knew her son was a genius. The next day he was presented with a complete set of oil paints and an easel. A newly hired drawing-master was in attendance.

I'm a bit disturbed by other aspects of Mozart's childhood: so much tribulation, and so many petty obstacles to his genius. Mrs Mozart would read the kind of Germanic fairytale trash to him when he was impressionable that I wouldn't read to my dogs or cats.

And Colonel Mozart, that superstitious old Mason, fed him a lot of high-flying mysticism mixed in with racy accounts of episodes on the Rhine in the Hundred (or was it the Thirty) Years' War. The child Mozart was himself living in a peaceful city though there was a Cold War going on involving I think the Holy Roman Empire and some other empire that had little use for Holy Romans. I'll look this up later.

MOZART FACTBOOK

Wolfie himself detested flutes and this I trace back to his childhood and the conflict stirred up unwittingly in the young genius by Colonel Poldy Mozart, who drunkenly broke into the Papageno nest and interfered with Marie-Antoinette, while the young Wolfie was perfervidly mixing burnt ochre on his brand new palette.

It so happened that, just at that time, a beggar was playing a flute in the street below. Later, when Poldy sent for the beggar in order to reward him handsomely for the musical accompaniment, he found that the man had mysteriously vanished. A certain Professor Koechel, just then passing by on his daily walk, was asked to help run down the beggar. But in spite of Koechel's exertions the man, with his haunting music, was never found.

When Wolfie was seven years old, while they were suffering through a bad winter in Salzburg, Leopold decided that his son, obviously a genius, would have to learn something about the ways of the world. So he got his son a job as a newsboy for the *Salzburger*

Zeitung. Every day before dawn the child genius is awakened by the eleven-year-old but already blooming sister Nannerle and given a hot cup of chocolate —

> *"Choco-late, choco-late,*
> *You must not be-late, be-late!"*

— and then he hitches up his little Shetland pony, fills the pony-cart with *Salzburger Zeitungs* and away they go —

> *"Pony-cart, pony-cart,*
> *That must be Little Mo-zart!*
> *Little fart, little fart!*
> *Mo-zart, Mo-zart!"*

— bells jingling mournfully in C minor to do the paper route. At first Mozart finds the winter mornings almost unbearably cold, and, what is more annoying, he is rarely skilful enough to hit the front porches of the sleeping burghers' homes with the first throw. Dazedly, the child who would later manage amorous pre-dawn assignations with Countess Zerlina and hundreds of other women (like his own Don Giovanni!) with astonishing alertness and flair, climbs down from Zerlina's stout little back (for Zerlina is the pony's name, a mere coincidence thrown up by history) and trudges up the snow-covered walkways to retrieve his bad shots — the newspapers that fall into the bushes or into the moats or into the cisterns of drowsy pre-dawn Salzburg.

I can't bear to think about it — Mozart, Wolfgang Amadeus Mozart, forced at such an age into such unworthy work. True we have only the questionable authority of the omnipresent Professor Koechel on this circumstance. As usual, walking past the Mozarteum at dawn on one of his insomniac perambulations, he got a close look at what was going on. He saw Nannerle, and the pony-cart, and the cup of chocolate, and put it all together. Mozart was a common newsboy!

From Koechel's field notes we have also the sole accounts of

Mozart at summer camp, Mozart learning to play snooker at the YMCA, Mozart sliding down the laundry-chute of the Mozarteum, Mozart traipsing the back lanes with his dog Chopsy (short for Chop-sticks, a cross-breed, mostly Alaskan husky), Mozart skilfully fly-casting in a trout stream later immortalised by Franz Schubert.

For the peripatetic Professor Koechel, "the conjunction of the motifs of walking and insomnia reveals the meaning of each. Walking does not express the freedom of spirit, its ability to skim over the surface of things and break away from the changelessness of matter. Oh no! It signifies instead man's inability to escape from himself."

And so I too would walk the Boulevard Raspail, the many streets of Doreen, for the millionth time perhaps, to encounter the unfocused resentment of my ex-wife Maisie and her sinister, violent second husband Boris. And dreaming of the distant, ailing Margot. My robust frame seen at night in all suburbs, all the expanding suburbs of "the city of tear gas", sleeping beneath its Carpark Tower. I transected the squares, the parkways, the ovals, the crescents, the terraces, the stoops of the lowly, the gardens of the Governor-General. My insomnia testifying to a "mind that is contradictory or impossible" and yet for me somehow real...

I sat in all the cafes on all the sunny afternoons of the sunny season and during the rainy season I sat before the fires laid for me by indifferent hostlers where I could sip the purple Doreen wines or my more bracing national drink, the dry martini. My concealed micro-cassette recorder tallying up what passes for conversation among the townsfolk.

Haunted by my insomnia.

Mozart contracted his insomnia the night he returned to the little Papageno nest — he had been listening to a beggar playing a little tin flute in the street below — and found it vacant. Marie-Antoinette had flown the nest, apparently, the torn linen testifying to the ravages of Colonel Mozart as he overran the frail defences of the frightened child. Later the kindly old Colonel sold her to a Turkish officer, who in turn sold her to the King of France.

She outlived her childhood companion by two years, two wonderful years full of incident and amusement.

Mozart threw himself into the Papageno nest all ceremonially stripped as usual and lay still for hours; hours announced by the grim old clock above the fireplace where his grandfather the General's grizzled likeness was ostentatiously hung. The dawn's first-light found him wide-eyed, knees drawn up, legs clasped by frail arms, in the identical posture I have often seen you, my Margot, assume.

This Mozart, who "could compose so long, so fluently, so aimlessly without the slightest sign of fatigue", could now be seen sitting still for hours without stirring his hams.

Not even an eyelid stirred.

The Mozarts are leaving the old house at 625 Forty-Second Street, Salzburg. Poldy has been promoted by the Holy Romans to Most General Officer and the new establishment will have to be closer to Rome or Paris, if not both. Soon, Poldy shows his boy to the Pope, who knights him, age eleven. But that is nothing, the Pontiff had done the same thing for the irrepressible Glueck only a few weeks before. The Pope liked knighting little boy-geniuses. Leopold tried thereafter to persuade Wolfie to sign his already burgeoning correspondence "Chevalier Amadeo", but this makes the democratically minded Wolfie want to retch. And he has not forgotten "the Antoinette", her wan little body, and he doesn't even have her address any more now she's in the land of the Turks.

His sister Nannerle begins to assume new importance for him.

Prior to the departure of two of its members for the newly expanding city, Paris, the Mozarts have a last dinner together *en famille*. They eat Mrs Mozart's famous buttered parsnips, parsnip pie, and finally toast smeared, much to the boy's delight, with parsnip jam.

Leopold would never see his beloved wife again: she would die in

Paris and the spare, stricken Amadeus would be the only one to return. Nannerle would stay to care for her father, catering to his whims, and serving, occasionally, as a physical solace. This is according to Koechel who sometimes dropped in at the Mozarteum during late evening walks. Even the jaded aesthete and citizen of the world is appalled by what he supposes to be the excesses of the Mozarts; father and daughter evidently vying to outdo one another in wantonness.

Leopold would hold forth arrogantly on his theory of incest. Incest was enjoying an unusual vogue in those times, but Leopold went so far as to link the practice with the very origins of creativity itself. He was making a religion out of an innocent social practice.

"In-cest creates in-sight," was his self-satisfied way of putting it.

My chapter on Leopold is difficult to write with tact, delicacy. I decide to knock off for the day. Reaching my house in the northern suburbs I throw myself on my sofa-bed. A sofa-bed is not as good a sofa as a sofa is. Nor is it as good a bed as a bed is. There is a parable in the sofa-bed. The sofa-bed tells the story of my life.

From the neighbourhood I hear the disconsolate cry of a child, followed by the wail of the divorced woman next door. My neighbourhood is populated with twenty-five-year-old divorced women and their pairs of children, one handsome boy usually slightly taller and wiser than the one pretty little girl, his sister. Occasionally there is drama when bereft ex-husbands attempt to steal these pairs of waifs back from their mothers. We had such an attempt across the street only last night, with quite a bit of gunplay and a number of methodical police and hysterical siblings. And the usual tear gas.

The body of the father was left on display in the front garden this morning. A warning to the other fathers who cruise up and down the street, mustachioed, in their new sports cars, waiting for a chance to steal back their children.

Leopold Mozart always made sure he had the law on his side. The robust twins presented him by Nannerle became his own property without question. They were part of his Grand Experiment with incest.

You see, Leopold was working on a new strain of genius.

Just as Mrs Mozart before her sudden unexplained death was working on a new strain of parsnip jam.

Neither succeeded for reasons that needn't detain us. The robust twins had, between them, an IQ that totalled a flat 200. No more geniuses have entered the world since the birth of Wolfgang, the little Chevalier Amadeo.

Conceived in lawful love, I hasten to add.

I am sitting in my office twelve storeys above Doreen in the dry season, indulging my old pastime of playing Monopoly against myself. Capitalism is charming in miniature, as a game! The board is laid out beneath the open window, and the play money, as colourful and plentiful as Australian money, is fluttering in the slight breeze. I am also thinking about my Mozart book. What I'll say — what I've found out.

My book on Mozart! The manuscript pages, too, fluttering in the morning breeze that somehow finds its way up here above the stately Carpark Towers of the city.

Walking into the Doreen Mall this morning, having got off the bus at the usual stop at the usual time, I notice somebody is finally cleaning the tiered fountain that stands at the centre of the mall, next to the equestrian statue of Leopold Mozart. Hoses coiling into the snotgreen water.

But — hey! The workman looks remarkably like Boris, Maisie's ex-CIA husband. He is pouring alum into the fountain and vacuuming the several tiers with the snakelike hose... Is he looking at me over his shoulder?

Boris has sworn to hunt me down, if only to prevent my publishing the Mozart book. This year the CIA regards Mozart as a hot item. Creativity, in the age of Star Wars technology, must be treated as a closely guarded secret. Whatever Mozart had...

whatever he tapped into . . . the CIA wants to know more about it before the other side does.

Already there is speculation that the Russians know about Leopold's abortive experiments with the twins.

And why were two armies, at the end of World War II, rapidly converging on Salzburg from opposite directions?

Why else, if not to retake the Mozarteum?

Passing the record shop. The manager's wife steps out to tell me — in a complicit whisper — that the new digital discs have finally arrived: Karajan's final recording of *The Magic Flute*. I shall play it in my office, twelve storeys above this smallish city.

And I shall take the precaution of using the headphones.

MOZART NOTES

Right now, Wolfgang Amadeus Mozart is lying on his back in a red toy wagon. He is gazing up at the ceiling, at the row of chandeliers in the long billiard room of his grandparents' house. Since it is raining outside and he is alone in the house, he has been toying with a child's innocent erection. Without knowing it he is spending a portion of the Hundred Years' War in this dreamy, indolent fashion.

Then he notices for the first time that rooms have — *ceilings.* He's been idly pushing the wagon around with his foot dangling down over the rim, just enough to touch the floor.

Later this child would seduce the flawless Countess Zerlina.

Now his feet barely touch the floor. Not so many years hence the shapely cannabis-scented lips of the proud Zerlina will seek his, her tongue ricocheting off his talented tonsils.

Lying in the red wagon, a gift from his grandpa, W. A. Mozart learns a new trick, genius that he is. A peculiar and powerful sensation can be created merely by blinking furiously! Turning Reality off and on as if it were an electric light. Suddenly it is as if he is *on the ceiling* looking *down* at the chandeliers, which appear to be *sprouting out of the floor* below. Up here with him, the billiard table and the little red wagon are as if bolted to the ceiling by a force greater than gravity.

For Mozart has discovered a new Force.

A Force — linked to the power of Music itself!

No longer is his body shackled to the wagon with the pressure of gravity — that boring, everyday, unquestioned presence. To break free of the wagon now would be to fall *downwards* onto the sharp protruding chandeliers below. Their elastic thrust — as if they could immolate a drowsy Genius.

But no — he's safe. He is learning *reversal of pattern* and this is maintained by harnessing the power of... some inexplicable ambience of the toy wagon, its radiance and special character counterfoiling the mundane force of gravity.

And this force works in *both directions.* Mozart gently releases himself from the wagon and drifts like a leaf fluttering in a breeze, downward to the ceiling. As he floats down, away from the earth, he glances about with a lucid, calm eye and sees a score of multi-coloured billiard balls in orbit around him, levitating with him, as in a spectral dance of matter.

Then how delicious for the child Mozart to reverse himself, to return softly to the transfigured world now above him. Maybe there's a pet dog up there, a cross-breed named Chopsy or, like my Skippy, a small cocker spaniel. How sweet, then, to leave the upside-down world and return to the world now of living and luminous matter and its prophetic artefacts, the Ming vase, the player piano, the Monopoly set.

The Monopoly set?

WAR DIARY

As a private soldier with Eisenhower's forces I was one of the first from our side to enter Salzburg. The smell of tear gas was heavy in the air. I took the tram, the old Martyrstrasse tram, to the Mozarteum. Hitler's armies had indeed beat a hasty retreat, for the door was wide open. A few street urchins were playing in the doorway.

I reflected, as I hurried past them, gaining the stairs, that they might have stood as models for portraits of the Little Chevalier himself.

I bounded upstairs to where I knew the Papageno nest must have been and threw open the closet door. As I rummaged through the musty costumes still hanging in there, I could hear their footsteps on the stairs, the guttural accents of our Eastern Bloc "allies".

I gave myself about one minute to complete my search.

It was then that I saw it. Under a heap of mouldy robes:

The red wagon that Koechel had described, and in it the anachronistic Monopoly set!

As the Russians stormed up the stairs, bayonets at the ready, clumsily skewering everything in sight as they looked for they knew not what, I sauntered past them on the stairs, the toy wagon under my arm. I stepped aside politely as the patrol stumbled past. I vouchsafed them a pleasant deferential wave of my free hand, as if to salute distant colleagues. When they got to the landing the squad leader stopped and looked back down at me, where I had paused on the staircase below them. He spoke a little English.

"Hey, GI Joe, I see you Yanks still like to play with toys, hey? Maybe later, when we big boys are finish here, I give you a ride in your little red wagon, hey?"

It was not a witty riposte, but, in his opinion, worth repeating in his own Slavic guttural to his men. They all stood there on the landing, pointing down at me: snickering, wheezing, roaring with laughter. While they were still slapping their meaty Slavic thighs, making catcalls, whistling derisively, I tried to exit with as much dignity as I could muster.

But then the squad leader noticed the Monopoly set I was holding. With a rude gesture he demanded I expose the contents of the box. When he saw what was inside he barked out an order in Russian and several men came clattering down the stairs towards me. Seeing the looks of Eastern bloc greed on their faces I upended the box and shook out the Monopoly notes, and as they fluttered down into the stairwell the whole squat squad of Russians tumbled rapaciously after, with only the hurried bayonet thrust or two in my direction as they passed.

Few things look more ludicrous than a mass of heavily armed men trying to race down a steep flight of stairs, abreast. They had not looked nearly so funny coming up.

"Buy yourselves a vodka, on me!" I shouted. Then I ran to catch the Martyrstrasse tram.

I knew that I — and perhaps Western Civilisation itself — had won that round.

Taking a sharp new pencil, W. A. Mozart sat down in the Paris house, in the intimate little study next to the Conservatory, and in fifteen minutes by the grandfather clock composed the "Fantasie in C Minor" for piano. Koechel Number 475. And how old was he then? To determine his age for any composition, you always take the Koechel number, divide by five and add ten.

Wolfie's mother was buried that morning.

It's not important but I have a touch of the flu today, or I hope it's only flu and not something more serious. I'm trying to work on the book but the type looks funny on the word processor, as if somebody has been tampering with my daisy wheel. And the world political situation complicates things too. I might be recalled to the Northern Hemisphere as promptly as I was dispatched down here, Down Under.

— Down Under what? Mozart might have said.

— And what happened to that red toy wagon?

I brought the wagon to Australia with me. It was an odd thing to present at the customs desk. It was an antique and therefore not subject to duty. Outside the Sydney Airport a number of protesters were forming up to attend a rally against a visiting American nuclear carrier. I walked past them, nodding my approval, Mozart's red toy wagon under my arm.

Riding the bus into Doreen this morning I had strange thoughts. Staring out the window at the sidewalk cafes, the stirring life of the city morning, not a time conducive to mordant visions, I found myself reflecting on poor Wolfie at last having to take his leave of history.

An ancient musician is summoned to the bedside. Mozart asks, in a failing voice, for something to cheer him up. Then why not his favourite music — the merry song of Papageno the simple birdcatcher? Eh? For a dying man?

But...say, *who is this guy*? He withdraws from the labyrinthine folds of his cloak a certain glistening instrument. And, rudely ignoring Mozart's dying request, he begins playing another piece from the same composition.

It is a flute melody. It is, in fact, the mysterious Magic Flute motif itself!

With a pitiable groan Wolfie turns to the wall.

He always hated the flute. His real love was the glockenspiel.

The first light finds Wolfgang Amadeus Mozart wide-eyed, knees drawn up, legs clasped by the frail arms, in a posture I have often seen you, my Margot, assume. This Chevalier Amadeo who "could compose so long, so fluently, so aimlessly without the slightest sign of fatigue", could now be seen — by the peripatetic Koechel stealthily departing —

Lying there perfectly still.

A Tartarus of Bachelors
and Maids

We burst into the room, an unruly collection of would-be roisterers. But we find Branstetter alone at the computer, playing chess with the Artificial Intelligence. The room has not been cleaned or aired for weeks. The woman who used to do the cleaning on Fridays refuses to come any more. There was a hoo-roar when her boss demanded outrageous favours. Branstetter is a dangerous, moody man at times. But he can tell a good joke. (Though never against himself.) We all think we would like to enjoy his success in life — without having to be like him in other respects. His mind is huge and shifty, like the legendary mountain Mam Tor — consisting of alternate layers of shale and gritstone.

"Jane the Drab", for that was how he styled the cleaning woman, got herself another bachelor, namely Darko DeWitt, meanest man in town. He grilled her jealously, hoping he had hired a clean, class-drab on the strength of Branstetter's recommendation. He wanted an all-purpose woman short of a wife. Would she . . . would she ever go to Branstetter again? Sure! Like every second Friday of the week.

Breathing out our ethylated fumes, we gather round him at the VDU monitor. The canny old Artificial Intelligence is temporarily winning, but Branstetter will let it come close and then, hitting the switch, he'll toggle himself into the winning position. The Intelligence will work its arse off preparing the way for its own defeat. Is there a moral in this? Thus are reserved for Branstetter all the reciprocal kicks of winning and losing.

"Listen — because us so-called human beings ultimately seek pleasure we shall always defeat the Chip. Ever seen a Chip with a pair of balls, mate?"

From such poetry, and in the last extremity, Jane the Drab, a divorcee with a kid to support, had fled to Darko DeWitt. Mumbling his Gauloises, DeWitt had looked her over not in an unkindly fashion, though as always preserving the winsome air of arrogance. He would get his four hours of scrubbing out of her and then she would cut the lunch and then, of course...

Darko extracted some passing pleasure from the Drab, he admitted, years later, thumping his creaky old wheelchair at the memory of what could be no more. I was dubious but preserved silence, remembering the Pixies, who had done him the year before the Drab. Then, unfortunately, remembering my Supreme who had done him the year before that. Who was using whom? And before that the actual wife, an ancient mistake.

Branstetter's MA thesis on The Aesthetics of Neo-Freudian Feminism lies open on the modular desk, there for the quick eye to spot, heavy as the very Stuff of Thought itself. In our competitive game it is enough to give a person the sweating sickness to see all those rival pages mounting up — piles of cowflop for all we know, with our unreliable eyesight. And he's writing a lot faster since the Drab deserted him for Darko.

In two more moves, just before checkmate, Branstetter trades games with the Intelligence — just in time. Now, with the Intelligence hanging on the ropes he can give us his full attention.

So Uncle Jake unflaps his weathered brown bag and out comes the flagon sherry, a short measure just to stave us off until more serious drinking will — *must* — set in. Unspeakably filthy tumblers are handed round. The sherry tastes like grandad's socks, and does Jake no credit. But it goes down more quickly for all that.

It is another summery afternoon in the city of Doreen, but not one to inspire confidence in the Maker. There is no cricket match on the TV. Supreme has strict orders to ring me at Maison Branstetter when something — anything — starts happening, anywhere. Even a free puppet-show in the park.

The very thought of Supreme is like crossing a graveyard at midnight. Or, to change the metaphor, our relationship is growing stale as a bureaucrat's bum. Or, to change the metaphor again, a mean old wind, a mean dry pampero of a wind, is blowing through us both.

I always wax poetical thinking of Supreme.

As Uncle Jake apologetically snuffles the sherry, we have him on a bit about his predilections and then we have Branstetter on a bit about his and then it seems proper to go, before they have me on a bit about mine; but for some reason we hesitate and the talk does not smarten up but we bolster ourselves anyhow we can and in what order we can seize, with another finer bottle that belatedly comes out from beneath the cowflop on the modular desk. More easily than most mortals, Branstetter can, in a twinkling of an eye, draw luxury from filth.

For some reason, none of us (it is late in the day, late in the century) has much of a reason, just now, for going anywhere. But there's no dignity in hunkering down, either. No warmth in the pretence of failed genius. Howls of derision from somewhere...

The very next day after this aimless gathering, Supreme leaves me. Nothing personal, she says — it is just that she has decided to give up the companionship of males as such until she finds *herself*, until she discovers her own mission in this murky life.

"I must be here for some reason," she says.

I agree.

Then shortly thereafter I hear she is living with Branstetter himself, *typing his thesis*, I hear. That smarts! Another twist of the old kris.

Nevertheless, some time later again, during yet another temporary lull in my emotional and creative life — and just when I am thinking it will be time to be up and doing again in the Real World — I find the crestfallen Supreme herself at my door again, just in time for dinner.

I take her in, along with a couple of tons of laundry she has accumulated living at the Women's Shelter (whence Branstetter had driven her in fear and loathing at last). So for many a day after I am out in back, behind the fowl-run, like a raisin in the sun, thrashing the crusty stains out of everything she owns.

To show her I still care? Would I know my own motives?

Meanwhile, just about every day she hangs about inside the lean-to with gossips of her own sex, ranting endlessly to such as Jane the Drab about an indignity that had been offered herself in, say, 1977, by a perfect stranger.

"You know what the dummy hand is, in bridge?" Branstetter asks us, at our final pissup. He is on his way to an assistant professorship in Kentucky or Idaho. The Big Time. We do not (visibly) take umbrage.

"Some people live their entire lives as if they were playing the dummy hand. To them, everything is done by 'other people'. As if some little gnomes and pixies are sitting around at this folding cardtable playing the game of *your* life! To the Dummy, Life itself might as well be in Morse code. You get the score-card after you *die,* man. You know what I mean?"

"Yes, *kemo sabe,*" murmurs Uncle Jake, who has been drying out for the last few months and is not in a good humour.

I know some of us are thinking of our old mate Darko before the Pixies had come on the scene and maybe about Darko after they were through with him and after Supreme had done for him and when Jane the Drab had begun her little Morality Play (with his *cojones* representing opposed virtue and vice). And maybe Uncle Jake is thinking about himself. And maybe I am thinking about myself. And maybe about Supreme, too.

Branstetter flicks the switch and the Artificial Intelligence takes the back seat once again and then he ups the ante and tries the Level Three setting which gives him a Grandmaster's game. We will leave before he tastes the pleasure of this victory.

"All this good fortune in my life — which I am sure you, my good mates, revel in as much as I do — is almost enough to lead me into galloping Sabaism," he says, with a satisfied smile.

Adding with a kindly parenthesis, "I mean *star-worship,* of course. The only true religion of the late twentieth century."

Nobody says anything. Branstetter lights his pipe and we know he is about to think up a new Great Thought of the Western World.

When I get back to the villa I can hear Supreme's throaty voice:

"The first time I ran to him it was pure necessity, call it raw need, but it was still a false move, a copout." Hostile glances when I enter. ("Thou art the — Man!")

Could they be talking about *me* this time? Do I matter that much?

Then I remember I have been keeping them waiting for dinner. Supreme can be mad as a smoked wasp when dinner is late, and, if I don't watch my step, I as an employed person will be up for taking them all to the Zen Curry House.

In the background, on Supreme's new compact disc player, Linda Ronstadt is singing "Desperado".

I go to the sink and start peeling potatoes. Being slightly drunk, I start sadly remembering my other life. My parents overseas, my kids — wherever *they* are this year . . .

Where has Love gone, and has it gone forever?

And then, for no apparent reason, I recall a scene from a movie in which Brigitte Bardot has to assassinate an arrogant Mexican general. She carries a tiny cartoon-like bomb, but she cannot fire the wick: her delicate little silver Ronson cigarette lighter keeps sputtering out on her. Enemy troops — fat, boisterous Mexicans with rude unshaven faces — are closing in on her. Her blouse is torn from one shoulder. She's running out of time.

Suddenly her lover, who happens to be safely hidden in a nearby tree, notices her predicament. Taking careful aim at the general's huge black cigar, he shoots it out of his fleshy, self-indulgent mouth. The cigar rolls to Bardot's feet. She picks it up with trembling fingers and manages at last to light the fuse. With an awkward elbow-forward throw she takes out the general and a few dozen troops in the bargain. Look of astonishment on the fat unshaven face of the general. Looks of astonishment on the fat unshaven faces of the troops...

Meanwhile, Supreme is telling Jane the Drab (*sotto voce*) how unworthy she was, then, to be called a human being.

But she has found herself now, she says. And now she is ready for the next step. Supreme has been offered a research assistantship.

"In Kentucky, or Idaho or somewhere like that," she says, now raising her voice loudly enough for me to hear it.

It occurs to me then that my old mate Branstetter might be a first-class bastard.

"What do you think about going to the Zen Curry House tonight?" I hear myself saying in an upraised, shaky voice.

LAST EXIT TO LAGUNA BEACH

He wakes up by stages, climbing out of dream within dream. He is surprised to find he's still alive, for in one of his dreams he was blown away — murdered. The Jewish Toy Merchants of San Francisco, losing patience with him for not finishing everything on schedule, had sent a woman. Sure, they knew it was not his fault, but they were losing thousands of dollars every day that production of the COPYCAT was held up. It was time somebody was taught a lesson. She had rubbed him out in a most considerate way. Still, he didn't like having to die.

But he wakes up to a bad dream, too, only it's called Reality — which is to say a bad dream with all the continuity written in. And . . . there is a girl beside him! His ex-prizefighter's instincts tell him it's not his wife — she's back in Scarsdale for a few days . . . weeks . . . months. The pressure on her was getting a bit much. A professor's daughter who did honours classics at Swarthmore could not be expected to thrive in the world of business. That's why Brad had resigned his Vice-Presidency on the East Coast — in a very big concern — and moved to California. If nothing else the climate would do her some good. Anyway, they'd buy a place with a pool and lie in the sun. But the competition on the West

Coast was unbelievable. He'd done a bootstraps operation and set up a little engineering concern from scratch. A few of his best boys from the East had been talked — bribed — into following him West.

Braintree, the best plastic fabrications man on the East Coast, led the gang who'd made the big shift. They all were a little afraid of California. It was like being at a jungle outpost on the edge of darkness. So they all bought houses on the same street in Laguna Beach. That way they could keep in close touch, day and night. They were going to stay a team.

Before they were able to get furniture in their houses, or grass seed down (or chlorine in their pools) they were hard at work. They began by designing assembly lines for small manufacturing concerns and then they got into installation of assembly lines and then they decided, what the hell, they might as well jump into manufacturing one hundred per cent. They knew plastics like nobody else in town.

So they started a few product lines on contract from certain retailers. The company name changed from Bradson Engineering to Bradfax.

At first circumstances conspired to help Bradfax get off the ground. It so happened that Brad's wife had some old school friends in Southern California. Once debutantes, they were now single professional women, forming a close-knit group, into radical politics and heavy feminism. (One day Brad had to pick up Penelope at Jane Fonda's house, but he had avoided going in — he just waited outside, revving the Pinto. Before his wife came to his rescue, he was hassled by Fonda's security guard.)

And then the contracts started rolling in — from Penelope's friends, in fact. The first ones: bubble packages for motivational cassettes ("So You Want to Help: Woman's Guide to Minority and Third World Investment Packages") and plastic buttons printed with slogans ("WOMEN WHO STRIVE TO BE EQUAL WITH MEN LACK AMBITION"). After a time, more fringe groups in Southern California were using Bradfax for their promotional materials. For instance, the Chicano Community Festival commissioned Bradfax to make half a million plastic tortillas, stamped with revolutionary slogans and equipped with the aerodynamic properties of the frisbee. Some of these floated as far as Laguna Beach, to the dismay of the little team, who felt compromised by their new vocation. It was not pure science any more.

And then Braintree disappeared, with a hundred and fifty thousand bucks, and the heady winking noon wine all turned to vinegar.

Brad rolls over and the girl stirs. She's young and . . . good God, he recognises her! She's Braintree's eldest daughter (Midge, Mamie?). He had sent her a Sweet Sixteen present when they still lived in the East. She throws a well-tanned leg over his thigh. California changes your life.

Later, after she has gone, the phone rings. It is Brennbaum himself, the Toy Merchant. Brennbaum always means business. A guy named Cozy Cousins vanished last year and the disappearance was laid by almost everyone at Brennbaum's door. Then Cozy's . . . uh . . . *remains* were found lashed to a paling on Laguna pier — and they were very untidy. Lots of not-so-nice things had been done to Cozy before he had finally snuffed it. The Coroner's Inquest of course ruled it death by suicide. When Brennbaum's toy business suffers, other people get to suffer too.

Okay, so maybe Brad's just being paranoid. Maybe Brennbaum is harmless, just an irascible old bee-jeeper and heaps of malicious folks are talking out of the wrong sides of their mouths. Sure, sure!

Brennbaum — a.k.a. "The Philosopher" — reputedly knows the works of Sartre and Camus by heart. Reputedly subscribes to a highly idiosyncratic theory of Reincarnation based on mathematical concepts of Probability. A self-styled authority on what he calls the "Big Picture". In short, a dangerous man.

— Listen, schmuck, how come you always keep on the wrong side of the metaphorical shithouse door, Brennbaum hisses, over the phone. And that's not a question, by the way. And now you make another mistake and you climb into a little blonde shiksa. Not to worry, not to worry — she's clean. She just told me all about it on the phone, in tears. What kind of a man are you? Just because her father crossed you. What is more, she thinks she loves you, even though I *paid* her to surrender her sweet little tocus to you. So now I take her off the case, send her back to Bryn Mawr to study Business Ethics. May I tell you the story...

— Brennbaum, excuse me but I can't help feeling paranoid. I told you that girl's father absconded, defaulted on me, left me a hundred fifty K in the hole and I've found no way to finish rewiring the assembly line. I got to scare up some money to cover the short-term costs. Otherwise, they won't even turn on the electricity at the Laguna Plant! How else are we going to get the COPYCATs into production? For chrissakes, Brennbaum, try to see my side for two minutes!

— In two minutes I can tell you a story, kid. About how they took the flea-ridden cur which was given unto them and they dressed it and they called upon the name of Baal from morning even until noon, saying O Baal, hear us. But there was no voice, not any that answered...

— Brennbaum, forgive me but I don't see what you are getting at. Braintree, my best man, has left me, absconded, and I wake up with his daughter this morning and ask myself what she is *doing here!* I'm a happily married man.

— *And they leapt upon the altar which was made,* Brennbaum said. *And it came to pass at noon that the Prophet mocked them, and said cry aloud for he is a god; either he is waiting, or he is pursuing, or he is on a journey...on a journey,* my friend!

— Brennbaum, it is *already* the middle of the day. I have bad dreams, and I can't even sleep right any more. I miss my loving wife in Scarsdale, and if the pressure doesn't ease off soon I can't meet any of my obligations. I have been living on Ricco's pizza special for six months and I've put on a small but noticeable potbelly and I can't find time for jogging any more. The neighbours are getting suspicious of my lifestyle, and then somebody sends that young kid over. And then... and then Ricco puts too many anchovies in his pizza and the salt is raising my blood pressure!

— And they cried aloud, and cut themselves after their manner with knives and lancets, till the blood gushed out upon them...

The phone goes dead.

Brad faces another day of trying to wriggle out of his little spot. He can either get the assembly line cranking or... or take the long walk.

Think about it, though. Isn't it basically a matter of getting the rewiring done *real* soon? But of course that takes money — in round terms forty thousand bucks! His options are pretty minimal. Like, he *could* try to rent out his two empty warehouses in Santa Monica. He'd worked on that idea night after night, sitting in Ricco's pizza parlour, soaking up "the Beer that Made Milwaukee Famous".

But Brad will *need* both warehouses if ever the assembly line does get cranking. Which means that if he rents them out to somebody else right now — in a matter of only a few weeks he will once again be up Old Bullhead Creek. For who would rent a warehouse to *him*? He'd made exploratory phone calls to other manufacturers, but no dice, they said. Bradfax was crashing a game where they once called the shots. Let the Jewish Toy Merchants help prune the competition. Like Cozy Cousins he would have to wear the suit. That's showbiz, folks!

The COPYCATs are already being advertised in the F. A. O. Schwartz Christmas catalogue and orders are pouring in. But nobody has seen anything yet but the Prototype released for promotions. Braintree himself had made the Prototype by hand so as to determine the assembly-line parameters. It was left for safekeeping with Brad. He had gone out one day for his usual run on the beach with his dog Americk (o Americk!). Coming home he found that the Prototype was missing! Howls from Brennbaum.

Shock/horror reactions from everybody else in the city. Braintree had preserved a prolonged silence — contemplating his defection no doubt. That was the only Prototype. The key to the assembly process!

COPYCAT is, well, the *ultimate* toy. COPYCAT (whose precise formula is a secret closely guarded by wise Toy Merchants in the city of San Francisco) is light-years ahead of the computer, which merely *relays* to children the thought-processes of adults. It is basically not much more than a stripped-down three-dimensional solid-copying device, but it has the potential to make kids independent of adults forever — almost. For COPYCAT will not copy itself — and that is where Bradfax comes into the picture.

Small wonder, then, that Brennbaum offered a reward of twenty thousand bucks, no questions asked, on the return of the Prototype, which, if it fell into the wrong hands...

Bear in mind that, technically speaking, Bradfax is involved only in packaging COPYCAT. The high-tech bubble plastic container is itself a marvel of design, and superficially COPYCAT is *all* container. The ''contents'', the active ingredients, are supplied by the wise Toy Merchants at the bottom of the assembly line, and Bradfax doesn't know how they are made, if they are ''made'' at all. Bradfax merely reserves a region within the package for the proprietary AM (''Ark Module'' — so named in keeping with the Talmudic interests of its distributors). The missing Prototype was, unfortunately, primed with an AM.

Brad drives into Laguna Beach for a midday pizza, racking his brain for solutions. As he pulls up in front of Ricco's Pizza, he notices a kid standing next to the parking meter. He gets out, carefully locks his Porsche as she approaches him.

— Gee mister, that's a nice car. You used to run on the beach, didn't you? With your dog. Then one day he ran away from home, didn't he? I know what happened to him. Do you want to hear?

Poor Americk! Wretched mutt! Brad had missed him that day after their jog on the beach, had scoured the neighbourhood (for a few intense hours) but had finally been too busy — hunting for the Prototype, in fact — to continue the search. Another casualty at Brennbaum's door. And Brennbaum had taken a special liking to Americk, had often asked after him. Well, there's no point now in knowing what happened to Americk. Too painful. A dog couldn't survive near those freeways, with all the juvenile delinquents driving around in their souped-up taco wagons.

— What do you do at the beach every day, kid? Don't you know it's dangerous to hang out there by yourself?

Brad notices she is wearing old-fashioned *polio braces* on her spindly legs, like some kid out of the pre-Salk vaccine era. She is also wearing a nylon stocking like a little skull cap on her head, reminding Brad of the ringworm he caught when he was a kid. She has lost a lot of hair, too. Poor kid! I wonder who lets her play at that beach?

Brad has to have his pizza.

But he is thinking about his own childhood for a change. He remembers his first dog, Skippy the spaniel. Did Cozy Cousins ever have a pet? Of course he did. Did Brennbaum ever have a childhood? Of course he did.

Did Braintree ever have a daughter?

Somehow, odd result of thinking about his childhood, Brad decides to take a chance. There's really no other way out. A few phone calls and it turns out that Toxicon Products (whom he has kept at bay in the past) will lease his warehouses, and from that he can raise half the necessary cash, if only to put off the day of reckoning. It is three in the afternoon. Abe Linckitts of Toxicon is not an agreeable man, and he's evasive when asked what he will be storing in the warehouses. Never mind, let the insurance people sort that one out. I need another twenty — today — Brad thinks. He deposits the cheque from Toxicon at the Laguna Beach automated teller. The die is cast — but I'm not going to be the one to die.

Four o'clock: he takes another chance and rings up Rob Burns at

Burns Electrical. This is one of the shonkiest concerns in Orange County. Sure, Burns has taken people for more rides than Disneyland, but Brad cannot afford the luxury of dealing with fully honest types. Honesty costs money around here. Burns Electrical had got their quote for wiring the assembly line down to twenty thousand. The materials themselves would come to ten. Brad knows where Burns will get them but doesn't want to think about yet another day of reckoning: like when somebody finds out that the Sisters of Mercy Hospital — due to receive its first patients in a few weeks' time — is entirely without internal electrical cable on the upper two floors. And nobody will know it — until the first doctor plugs in the first cardiac monitor.

Burns recruits its tradesmen from among Asian refugees, on the premise that anyone sharp enough to rig up anti-personnel explosives for the ARVN — and to live long enough to make the escape to America — deserves new opportunities in the land of the free. Burns Electrical, please note, can afford to lose one or two wiry little electricians per week to industrial accidents. Since all Burns employees work illegally, their survivors are reluctant to lodge claims for compensation.

Rob Burns keeps Brad in suspense for a while on the phone, while checking with the bank about Brad's deposit. Brad's cheque to Burns will clear (assuming that, in its turn, Toxicon's cheque to Brad will clear) and so the electrical team will start work at the Laguna plant first thing in the morning. Now all Brad needs is a twenty thousand deposit for the Orange County Electrical Commission. Obviously, if the team shows up on site at six a.m. and the juice isn't turned on, another legendary substance will hit the fan. Goodbye Laguna Beach, hello Laguna pier!

The Porsche was a good investment after all: it is fast. At four-thirty Brad is at the Commission with a cashier's cheque for the deposit. He is gambling on the possibility that Burns Electrical will wait at least until ten the next morning to present his cheque to the bank. By then Brad could be there with another twenty thousand to deposit. He'll have the whole night to come up with that twenty. If not . . . well . . . uh . . . try to get a good night's sleep. And there's still time for the Last Supper.

Ricco's Pizza, Laguna Beach. Six o'clock. If you know Ricco's you know that the man sitting in the corner, back to the wall, is eating the special, which can be distinguished by the veritable school of anchovies swimming across it. Like a parable of Loaves and Fishes.

Ricco's has this underwater motif, in keeping with its choice pierside situation. Heavy fishing nets, supplied by Ricco's brothers in the fishery fleet, dangle from various posts and beams. Drink too much of Ricco's Schlitz (on tap) and you might find yourself stumbling into one of these nets, bringing the lot of them down over you. And take care to avoid the fully primed and loaded Arbalete speargun. Ricco is an avid sportsman and usually catches enough fish and squid to make his pizza marinara the Best in the West. We might add, as an anecdote of local interest, that it was Ricco who discovered the remains of Cozy Cousins.

Ricco's pizza has to be tasted to be believed. John Wayne used to drive all the way from Palm Springs when he got the craving for it. And later, when the Duke was dying of cancer in UCLA hospital, he would dream night after night of a visit to Ricco's. Forget it! — Ricco never makes deliveries.

Smiling broadly, his Mediterranean good nature blooming as ever, Ricco brings Brad another pitcher of Schlitz. The little girl sitting with him is drinking an orange juice through a long plastic straw, sort of like the straws you get in hospital. Which, considering her anachronistic polio brace, seems appropriate.

She is telling him about the band of children she lives with. It appears they are squatters in an abandoned house near the beach. A flight of wooden steps leads from the house down to the sea. In winter they gather driftwood for their fires, while in summer they often sleep on the beach, to catch the sea breeze. They can see the whales on their northerly migration and hearken to the eldritch songs of the dolphins. They are indifferent to danger. They know that no harm will come to them, isolated as they are. Unlike poor Brad, they sleep peacefully at night.

— And we have a dog, she says slyly. We found him on the beach. Perhaps...would you like to meet him?

— Somebody has to take you home, my dear, Brad says. Ricco waves at them as they leave. *Arrivederci!* You bet, Ricco!

The dog (of course!) is dear old Americk, good old slavering Americk, the once-pudgy Labrador, a one-time lover of pizza crusts. Living with the children has given him a slender new dignity, and an expanded status as dog-of-the-place. But his erstwhile master thinks he sees, in Americk's greeting, an occulted message.

The children lead Brad up to the attic of the old house.

— This is where we like to play dress-up, the girl says.

It seems the children often amuse themselves by plundering abandoned tea chests and cupboards in the creaky old attic, sometimes finding strange paraphernalia. (Brad now understands the polio braces, and the outmoded child's dress she wears. And why she looks like a ghost from his own past.)

And Brad finds something else. Americk tugs at his sleeve, leading him over to it.

Yes, folks, there on a mahogany wine table rests — sure enough! — the Prototype itself.

Gleaming now like the Holy Grail.

Have these innocent-looking kids been living by petty thievery? And...and why are they showing him this now? They wouldn't know about Brennbaum's *reward,* would they?

Well, it so happens (the charming little girl explains it, smiling up at Brad as if they had known each other forever) they "borrowed" the Prototype, so they could give it their *own* kind of quality-testing. Children can't be too careful about the toys they allow adults to make for them.

The kids wanted to know: was COPYCAT really fail-safe? So

they tested it for toxicity, submersibility, flammability, nuclear capability — you name it.

Now — uncharacteristically for him — even Brad wants to know what they found out. COPYCAT, after all, was a mystery to him too. (And yet, without thinking about what it might do to little kids, he had agreed to manufacture it for Brennbaum. So much for business ethics.)

Brad walks down the beach, meditatively, with dear old Americk following him home once again. He cradles the Prototype in his arms, thinking about his new friends, that odd little cabal of precocious kids...

Before he left they had made him a nice hot cup of tea (with a little lemon, a little sugar). Before politely explaining to him just what COPYCAT is:

Everybody can relax. For, in a nutshell, COPYCAT is just another harmless addition to the dream house adults are forever, shamefacedly, building for their children.

And so now Brad is standing in his empty living room, at the telephone, trying to get through to his wife in Scarsdale.

SOUTHERN COMFORT

Prue is thinking again about the early days of Rushmore. About how long it took before he would...

At first he had been a man of proprieties, as befitted his ideas about his professional image. (Rushmore was always talking about "images". Like: "the image of the female".) Because Rushmore felt that as a professor he was important, his love life was also important and must appear decorous. But — being an American — his idea of decorum was itself highly bizarre.

Prue would play along with any line of his so long as she knew where she was, though in many respects Rushmore was a great unknown. What shadowy ideas were in there, jitterbugging away beneath his massive cerebral dome? In other ways he was as easy to decipher as an afternoon tabloid.

Let's see, it took Rushmore two months to *get ready* to board her, even though she had capitulated (mentally) after their first long lunch — er, actually after their first drink.

Eventually he consented to lovemaking, after a protracted ethical discussion of the pros and cons (many cons, few pros — her life story in a cocked hat) — followed by his wrangling with what appeared in the stygian gloom of her bedroom to be a candy-cane striped contraceptive. But Rushmore...well...couldn't manage it!

Okay, okay, relax everybody! He was...uh...afraid of getting herpes from her, he said. For, earlier in the evening hadn't she — during their Truth and Soul session — dropped her guard and owned to having had a few lovers before...? (In point of fact Prue was still discreetly carrying a couple of old friends on her books. And wasn't really sure how much Igor — but especially Mahood — put her at risk.)

That was in the good old times, when herpes was what lovers worried about.

Rushmore's Second Attempt occurred after another long lunch. Her shout was oysters (Rushmore sulky). His shout was a bottle of Great Western brut laced with Southern Comfort (Rushmore animated, confident). They had the rest of the day to themselves, a fine libidinous spring afternooon. Result: Rushmore once again disappointing. But though his "device" (the term was his own) would not "actuate" (term also his) he had evidently been well trained by American women — which is to say he knew about both clitoris and g-spot. (Some Aussie males had heard of the former — never the latter.) Indeed, he had previously lectured her about them very knowingly.

Rushmore claimed this time that his device, loitering there palely now, would never lead him into danger and the danger now was that he might be falling in love. His logic here being somewhat circular: he never had trouble "servicing" women he did not care about. But of course the categorical imperative both of ethics and personal hygiene required that he shun such women like the plague. On the other hand, the onset of radical caring was enough of a systemic shock to drive away all sensation from the libidinous zones. A phenomenon "so common among Western males that Freud wrote an essay on the syndrome". Rushmore smiled wryly, as if relishing the "double bind" ensnaring not only himself but, supposedly, all other males of the Western world.

What struck poor Prue as strange was not so much this analysis (which she was able to assess on its own merits) but her discovery that she in turn might be falling for Rushmore...

Hopefully this was just misplaced solicitude. She needed more proof, carnal assurance perhaps.

When would Rushmore finally deliver?

And just what is love? That's what she wanted to know. Prue felt humiliated by her own feelings.

Rushmore's lecture series was well under way by the middle of the year. Since Australia was "twenty years behind" America in Rushmore's field, he would be overworked for the two years of his stay. He might even have to remain an extra year in order to bring the entire nation fully up to date. This would entail postponing a key research project in one of America's centres. Thus while Rushmore was helping the developing country overcome the tyranny of distance, his own country would fall behind — Prue worked it out — by three years.

If Delphine had truly been Prue's friend she would never have introduced her to Rushmore.

She had originally met him at a New Year's party in the Hills, given by a Czech lawyer. The Czechs had made her drink so much (was it called *slivovitz?*) that she was not sure about everything that happened. She was there as a table stuffer, female filler. Delphine, recently divorced, was cultivating a noisy, dangerous social life. Delphine assured her that the Czechs were the most fun-loving people in the world. Which proved too true. The Czechs, who, while drinking copiously themselves, appeared to remain always cold sober, had her totally pissed within half an hour. The house was opulent, beautiful: several levels of sundecks for entertaining, pool and spa, perched on the hillside with a view of the city lights. The host a confident, charming man — and very appreciative of Prue!

And then she was dancing — and then sitting down to a magnificent supper of Slovak unpronounceables. Stuffed pancakes, evidently; potato dumplings, unquestionably — and chilled sweet red wines.

Then she was dancing again with a man she retrospectively assumes was Rushmore. Like everybody else they were sweating. Rushmore had huge black sweat circles under his arms — gahhh!

The irrepressible Delphine shortly thereafter set up a mad lewd lunch fuelled by Southern Comfort and champagne cocktails to help Prue maintain her toehold on the slippery facade of this visiting American professor. Prue knew she had to front up. At that period in history no unattached woman would have passed up a chance to know a loose academic. Provided he was not an entomologist.

Prue is thinking about many things at six a.m. The Italians next door are noisily up and about greeting the day and each other with uninhibited joy that they are still alive, that they have not been *poignarded* in their sleep or awakened to find themselves back in Calabria buried under the rubble of an earthquake. Luciano Pavarotti is singing "O Sole Mio" on somebody's radio...somebody who's fiddling with the dial...then it's Bing Crosby singing "White Christmas".

Prue ruminating, at six a.m, propping herself up in bed. Her man of the evening has slouched back to his wife. No, not Rushmore. Somebody she picked up on impulse (he looked embarrassed, out of place) in the "Tower of Rats Charmed by Music", a trendy pub. He had given her a qualified pleasure. Afterwards he warmed her for a few hours, tossing and turning next to her. She thought he might be running a fever. Until he blurted it out that he had a wife at home. He crept out only after they exchanged mutual pledges: that neither of them knowingly had a communicable disease.

Why the hell had Prue ever taken up with Rushmore?

A MISSING (DELETED) EPISODE

A few piquant kilobytes of text, which I accidentally deleted from WORDBLOCK (my wordprocessor) related the encounter — after a few months of separation — of Prue and Rushmore. The whole episode puts into question Prue's ability to take human affairs with a proper dose of seriousness. The encounter took place in a suburban store known as Hard Mart (no irony intended). Prue was shopping for a "designer" screwdriver set (no irony intended), one which would fix her sewing machine and, if possible, come in handy for major roofing repairs, and yet still look feminine.

The missing episode included a remarkable conversation Prue overheard between Rushmore and the attractive girl who works behind the Information desk. (My field notes confirm that she is a very pretty girl, grown a bit stouter now, no longer quite so credulous.) Here Prue got to peer into the abyss: Rushmore's "line", which, though simple in its premises and internal construction, could be stunning in its effect upon shopgirls, waitresses, barmaids, and — in later life indeed it would sway — nurses.

The missing account recorded in instructive detail how Rushmore's line worked. Something about asking for help in choosing a gift for his mother in Palm Springs (or Beverly Hills), and involving a confusion about the Australian terminology for certain luxury wares, such as "toilet water" and the semantic traps into which distinguished, affluent, foreign visitors could so easily and unwittingly fall. And then there was something about asking the girl to try on (or splash on) whatever the item was and then something about gift wrapping it. At which point credit cards spilled out of the wallet in gay profusion — temporary embarrassment for local currency — Diners Club, Visa, American Express (Gold Card), Member's Ticket for the New York Stock Exchange, chit from the bar of the Beverly Hilton, Member's Ticket (no irony intended, in the missing episode) for a French Winetasting Society, the

Gourmet's Club, Swiss bank account instruction leaflet, etc., etc.

In her effort to stave off the pickup (and to spare Rushmore late-night anguish with potentially herpic girls) Prue intervened with an equally disingenuous line of query to Rushmore's own.

Words passed among them — quite a funny exchange, I recall — which finally led to a retreat of the counter maid and a re-establishment of the connection between Prue and the professor.

WORDBLOCK has also swallowed the careful plotting and motivation that led the two potential lovers to the Botanic Gardens, where they visited the famous fernhouse. Since Rushmore had spent a year of his youth in the fern country of the Amazon collecting exceptional specimens, they had plenty to occupy themselves with. After a few intermediate steps, involving a cold chicken and Southern Comfort-cum-champagne lunch overlooking the fernhouse, the narrative took them back to Prue's townhouse...

In the course of this singular afternoon Rushmore began composing an impromptu poem:

> We sat outside the fernhouse
> Quiet on the bench
> Drinking still sad wine
> Trying to avoid
> Doing something interesting...

Now Rushmore's favourite music was (no irony intended) Mozart's "Magic Flute". An opera that's not for everybody. But every recorded version save the Klemperer was an abomination to him. He liked the Klemperer performance for its "redundant chastity", for its "spirit of joy", its "pure Singspiel quality". Unbeknownst to him, the assiduous Prue had managed to scare up a second-hand Klemperer in Sydney shortly after the Second Attempt with Rushmore.

So they reeled homewards from the Botanic Gardens, prodded by the conscientious guard, who relieved them of the empty bottle of Southern Comfort. Rushmore whistled the famous flute motif all the way home (shamelessly emphasising the vibrato).

Hold on! This is not the story of a mere seduction. You can read those anywhere... in the garishly illustrated tabloids of London or Istanbul, or the well-thumbed slickies in Palm Springs beauty salons...

The divine music of Mozart was filling the room. The lights of the city were spread out below them winking like an amber cryptogram of life. But our all-too-human flesh is engraved with its own symbolism. The lover will speak only of love, and the fish never knows when it rains... And does not the common harlot wait until dawn to play tennis?

A ministress of life and calculated loss, Prue lowers the offertory disc onto the turntable. Lurching blindly, drunk with Comfort and perhaps with Love as well, she hardly knows what she is doing. The professor drones on, his stumbling, hesitant voice improvising his poem, and thus only protracting the darkness of desire. The tip of his beard waggling goatishly in the half-light of Prue's room.

From next door she can hear the sighs of the Italians as they bid one another good night. *"Buona notte... buona notte signorina..."*

Are they crying out to her?

But now, as Mozart fills the room, a new darkness answers the flute-song as it enters for the first time, sweet and yet poignant, like a fine rain falling on snow.

Years later, sifting through Rushmore's notebooks, adaze midst the pathless thoughts of the professor (skittering crabwise across a yellowing page), Prue would stumble upon the very formula of the man. In the words recalling that one evening:

> *when you hear the sound*
> *it is already past*
> *and you hear it again*
> *passing the arch*
> *taking stride of stone*
> *and that is the sound of the flute...*

NIGHTMARE: IN THE RAZORBACKS

"You must decide, Bernardo — tonight!"

Pilar and I are sitting near the campfire, cleaning our weapons.

"I was just remembering that Lebanese restaurant we used to go to in the South."

"The 'Jerusalem Windows' — you liked it because it was BYO."

Just then Hendershot reaches us in his rounds of the camp. A falling-out between any of us might endanger the whole group.

"So here are my two best infighters. What do you say?" Hendershot would speak English with a certain awkwardness. But he was not awkward with a gun.

She gives him the kind of dark look that wouldn't normally qualify as a reply. But she reserves the full blackness of it for me.

Hendershot, scratching himself with his Smith & Wesson, is wondering about something again. It is always dangerous when he thinks at all. But no, he turns away at last. It's time to look to the fires. He shambles away and we can see his wound is still fresh on him. We can look at each other again, exchange glances.

I wonder if we are really a group, whether the struggle needs us all at the same time or whether we might not be better off as solo operators.

My old rival Pachito is over by one of the fires, stroking the kid's long blonde hair. Ulyses, a pathological madman, is sitting nearby reading a book one of our bosses had tossed to him as we had left the South country: *The Way to a Flat Stomach* ("The success or failure of your relationships is to some degree always decided by your looks. Start easy and stay easy. Take plenty of time to achieve your goal: marble flat midsection with well-defined transverse ribbing.")

At the fringe of the camp, of my consciousness, the parrots are fattening on the remains of the one killed earlier. Bone-eating parrots. Part of the moonscape we are fighting over.

"I'll always be with you in spirit, in my mind," I say to Pilar, maybe preparing my exit. I can feel the landmass behind us, most of it the incomprehensible territory we define politically as our once and future homeland. The Razorbacks. Nothing but a scape of hills — beautiful dangerous hills.

"You always could make me laugh, Bernardo," she says, "but for once you must decide." She stands up, pauses for a moment, looking down at me, and then moves away into the shadows.

Now Ulyses is trying to remember the punchline of the story he has started telling the partisans. Callous, stupid — the definition of an audience for such gross fables — they will not appreciate it if he runs out of steam too soon.

How far away is the base camp now? *Is* there still a base camp? None of the partisans would know. I look over at Pilar, restlessly gliding in and out of the shadows, dark and then light. I can still feel her touch, hands like the wings of moths in the dark. From here I can almost see the outline of our child in her.

I feel as if we all are pushing blindly against the envelope of history itself, our trek a move in the wrong direction. Local elections have brought only trouble — the disappearances, the tortures, the deaths. One of our friendly groups, the Disinherited, employing the rapes that no woman could speak of afterwards.

"This is what giving women the vote has led to," Pachito had said, laughing, on returning from one of their little parties.

The captured child turns towards me, eyes full of the adventure. Yesterday she had watched as Pachito shot her elder brother. Cleaning out that particular patch of suburbia seemed a useless exercise, though Hendershot felt we had to keep our knives sharp for the real action.

The parrots leave off for a moment. Looking quizzically, madly, into space. Perhaps something is moving towards us. Ulyses could jump for his piece, but it would too late. The fiddle-man, somebody's blind old grandfather, freezes, too, interrupting the partisans' favourite tune: a hymn of struggle and sacrifice, a borrowed anthem.

Miss Wharton wakes up with a sigh, no doubt surprised to be still alive. One of the bosses had given her to us. For a month or so we have been carrying her along. She knows she's just about used up. A chilly wind is sweeping down from the Big Razorback. I can see her dark nipples — through the light, expensive garment — hard as rock-crystal.

A pause. Silence. And then Ulyses shrugs, starts playing with a scratchy dyspeptic radio. Hendershot resumes feeding (or smothering) the campfire. Miss Wharton's diamond bracelet blazes in the firelight as she rolls over. Pilar is not in sight.

No, nothing. *There is nothing out there.*

Boredom and danger stir our nostalgia, as for a wanderer who sees a familiar face transposed to black or yellow as he perpetually crosses border checkpoints in faraway countries.

Even Pachito seems to be feeling the pangs of nostalgia (a contagious emotion). His hands linger over the body, the spices of his captive child. It is a reflective moment, in spite of our situation. Nobody felt we would be here for long. We have held on for months, not without hardships, close scrapes. Our difficulties could serve as argument for even the sternest measures against ourselves. But what if we can no longer remember what we hold dear? The parrots of the country are (maybe) a sign. They feed at night.

How long the pursuers (we fondly imagine them as blackbooted, muffled in balaclavas) will take is hardly a question now. Perhaps it will be before we reach the wretches who are our own quarry. Sometimes pausing, like now, we discover those few feelings that five years of skirmishing have not frozen up utterly.

It is as clear as day I will never see the kid Pilar is carrying. There will be movements out in the bush even if I am the only one who will choose to hear them.

Over there a youth is polishing his piece, oblivious. There will always be more brothers to jump into the fray.

I have never been good at deciding things. Perhaps that is why it is so easy to kill, to perform unrepeatable stunts.

To walk away from Pilar?

Pachito's child stares into the campfire and I am suddenly struck by the look in her eyes, which seems to argue her antiquity. Or is it her universality? In the other life, in the North, I had children, two daughters. Years ago, when I saw them for the last time, they were only five and seven years old.

Cry of the parrots. Something is rustling in the bush. Is it just someone of ours, out for a stroll?

"Bernardo."

She signals to me from out there. I have no choice for the moment but to follow. The shadowy greens turn to a darker green and then there are the black stones. Moving well away from the camp now, I can see her in the blackness. She is high-breasted in outline as she mounts the hill above me. Perhaps each man loves one such woman in his life. When you live with them in the cities, they never stay for long, as is according to their nature. But this one, Pilar, has the knowledge of our kid in her and it is a burden she understands no more than the night-parrots understand the blaze of the noon.

I climb up a little higher, working my way towards her, up now where the night seems paler, a reflection of the water we have come to. We can look down over the water and that is where we see the lights, the pinpricks of light that mark the progress of either our pursuers or the ones we are seeking out. We have no signals or watchwords, no way of communicating in either direction. All the groups tend to resemble one another in their disregard for protocol and in their willingness to fire on anything that moves.

"I love you."

"I love *you*."

If she decides to leave our group it will be my duty to prevent her. Or I will have to answer for her, for we are not that slack, yet. And if I try to leave alone she will have to sound the alarm. We are both valuable in our different ways, but Hendershot would not take this into account in finishing us off, one or both.

But probably just me. He would be thinking that would leave her for himself. But by the time he began to know anything about her it would be too late — for her, and for him, too.

They would both be lost to Pachito and Ulyses and the others. A few more traitors to throw to the parrots.

It is a moonlit night in the North, in Vermont, and the two sisters are sitting on the dock next to the old rowboat. The kerosene lamp is beginning to grow brighter against the night. Up the hill at the white frame house they can see their mother, aproned, in the kitchen window. The sisters are wearing light frocks and are beginning to shiver as the cold crawls up from the lake. The old labrador is snuffling around in the weeds behind them.

The elder girl is annoyed by mosquitoes but since the expedition to the dock was her idea she pretends to ignore them. So she watches narrowly, calmly, as a large mosquito lands on her little sister's neck . . .

She is trying to explain to her sister precisely what is happening tonight in the land of witches and fairies.

The witches and fairies live operatic lives and observe protocol endlessly, obsessively. They live in paradise but can't stop squabbling over little things. And the big things — love and princes and the magic moments — never seem to give them lasting peace of mind either.

The two sisters sit there, the one telling stories, the other, the younger, dreamily looking out across the darkening lake.

Pilar is pointing it all out to me: two sets of fires separated by the line of hills and the patch of water. It is beautiful country, the Razorbacks, our theoretical Homeland.

I stand beside her as we look down at the fires, the sparks of light, and we can hear the occasional sounds of men turning in their sleep, or the stifled laugh or cry, indistinguishable at this range. The wisp of a song rises from a camp, maybe just an old crone wheezing out a dirge for a lost son.

If we were to go over there together, to try to join a different bunch, that would be impossible, too, as a pair.

Yes, moving like moth-wings in the dark: that is Pilar, and I know she has made up her mind to walk on down to the other side. So I know what I shall have to undergo, for our kid, and perhaps for her as well.

At least I should touch her now in farewell.

But when I finally turn from my thoughts she is gone.

Two young sisters sitting on a dock, next to the rowboat, the old labrador snuffling in the weeds along the shore of the lake. The one child speaking endlessly as in ritual, the other silent. But the elder sister's narration — the witches and the fairies — seems to keep bogging down, no matter how hard she tries to guide the story on the decorous track from magic moment to magic moment towards true bliss. The obstacles just keep popping up from somewhere outside her story but she does not know where from. And it is exasperating that the Fairy Prince's face seldom comes quite clear and that when it does little sister cannot be made to see it properly.

He is smiling at them and his eyes are beams of love. That is the true face of the Prince, a face of infinite love. But she is afraid her little sister will never see the face of the Prince.

This is the saddest thing she can think of. That she might never glimpse the Prince's perfect, loving face.

HOT SERVE

I don't have to tax my brain to recall the day I vomited on my father's Sony voice-actuated tape recorder...

Friday afternoon: I am lecturing in my special area. My father, who has paid an unexpected visit to my (adoptive) part of the world, is in the front row of the audience, an otherwise provincial flock of some two hundred souls. I am fairly launched into my subject, which I know backwards — and forwards as well. My father is killing a few days between businesses. He has just finished selling what was left of North American Shipping and has not yet got the keys to Antipodean Securities. He is wearing heavy woollen stockings over his bathroom slippers — a sartorial solecism he knows will annoy me. He is still unable to forgive me for the way I had used — he would say abused — him in a story published a few years ago in the *New Yorker*. My father took legal action against the *New Yorker*. In addition he cut me out of his will and cancelled my membership in the Sons of the American Legion.

I begin to feel light-headed, some...uh...*substance* roaring through my bloodstream. My father's mistress is plainly bored with my speech. Forgivably, since she has no English. She and my father don't have any language in common, but they get along okay. At the libel hearing she defended him stoutly, but in her own language.

She is not ugly — indeed my father is to be commended for his taste. The nose is a torment, true, and the face pockmarked. I won't allude to the scar-tissue: the war in her country was no teddy bear's picnic. She was thought to be in collusion with the enemy. She had not, therefore, been well treated by the partisans of her own colour. The Sony is sitting on her lap. She's encased in furs plus a very short skirt, dusky thighs beneath the Sony. The only other noticeable feature is the pneumatic bosom which her furry costume — that's the word for it — barely holds in check.

I notice — why had I not remarked it before? — that my third wife Minnie is seated just behind her. My father will not speak to Minnie since it was her testimony that won the libel case for the *New Yorker*. She satisfied the court that what I had passed off merely as *fiction* about my father's activities was totally factual. So certain people who learned he had wronged them in the past felt free to sue him in turn and the Old Man underwent a veritable acupuncture of litigation. It cost him a couple of million all in: court costs, bribes, settlements by the old hollow tree in the light of the full moon.

Meantimes, discretion prompted my mother to withdraw to Bosky Dell, our New Hampshire farm. When it all blew over she again took up the reins of the family business (a private detective agency). Now whenever she is out on a case — behind the wheel of her Ghia Turbo — she causes a certain commotion among those townsfolk who overvalue life and limb. For, while most people drive with their eyes, my mother, being extremely nearsighted, steers by memory. And, since urban renewal, Hanover is not the city it was in her youth.

Earlier in the day (of the throwing up) I had joined my father for lunch at the Grosvenor. (The Doreen Hilton, where he usually stays when in this part of the world, was booked out for a symposium on The America's Cup: Marxist Alternatives.) Lunch was served on his private little balcony looking out over our capital. Doreen: a city my father disapproves of.

What was it we had for lunch that day? Oysters Rockefeller probably. That's what my father calls his diet lunch, when he's living on his credit cards. I recently found a photograph of my father run by the local newspaper. He is seated at lunch, glass of champagne in hand. The reporter mentions oysters — Rockefeller?

My father and I are quite a bit alike, though God knows our careers have taken off in different directions. We share the family nose, the family potbelly, the family satyriasis. These attributes can be traced in portraits that go back to the sixteenth century. There is a fox-hunting portrait (eighteenth century) of one of my ancestors in which the belly, the nose and, presumably, the satyriasis, can be seen profiled to advantage in the one frame.

This — this feeling of slight nausea is not unknown to me . . . but I really do fear I'm becoming unusually light-headed . . . I am just now starting to make the point to my — so far quiet and intent — audience that I know will bring a few of the "experts" in the room roaring to their feet. It always does. But my knowledge of my chosen area is unassailable.

II

Perhaps we had too much champagne with lunch. Minnie, not invited of course, was off shopping with Sophie, an old school friend who is visiting for the holidays. Sophie! A silken smouldering creature, who keeps to the guest area when I am prowling about the house. I think Minnie has given her a warning word about my predilections. Now she is sitting next to Minnie in the lecture room. Every so often Minnie gives her a nudge, a glance . . .

Do they really think they are *invisible* from here?

How naked, how exposed an audience really is! And yet it vainly thinks itself privileged: thinks it can see without being seen! It does not realise that, given the *uniformity* of a mass of people, fixed in place in straight rows of seats, the slightest gesture, the faintest irregular movement, is magnified in direct proportion to the number of people in the audience who are *not* performing the same action! In this case, in an array of some two hundred people, most of whom are inert, as if anaesthetised, any unusual action would be amplified two-hundred-fold. Example: that nicotine-stained fraud in the back row — Dr Barfstein, one of my bloodthirstiest professional (and sexual) rivals — thinks he is the best hid person in the room. How delighted he is by the quivering titbits he is conveying from his left nostril to his gaping mouth! *Bon appetit,* doctor!

Everyone who haunts the podium knows what an overt spectacle *he* makes of himself — the wretch, that is, who courts anonymity in the back row. Indeed it is far more private right up here at the lectern — it's really a quiet little backwater up here!

And now...I think I begin to understand these events at last — with a certain uncanny lucidity.

For is it not the indecent *visibility* — the gross and provoking *nudity* — of this particular audience (father, mistress, wife, rival...Sophie) that sways me now, that stifles me!

My father's mistress crosses her legs with the deafening roar of garments torn from the bodies of predatory animals...

And silently as silkworms move in moonlight, the divine Sophie uncrosses hers!

I lean forward and...catching my breath...

Two dozen — must be fresh *Sydney* oysters — on the half shell
  Half cup cooked spinach
  Bread crumbs
  Two tablespoons chopped bacon
  Parsley
  Salt
  Louisiana Hot Sauce
  ...Serve at once.

LITTLE MYSTERIES
OF OUR CITY OF TEAR GAS

PS

I'm enclosing under the same cover several short pieces discovered on the person of the nicotine-stained old fraud who used to occupy the villa in North Doreen, just opposite my poor sister. Perhaps you will be kind enough to glance through them in an idle moment. They appear to be merely fictional. *That is, I do not think there is hard evidence or even any truth in them...*

As ever,

B.

I.

AMONG MY LAVENDER LADIES

I am dozing off in the back garden, a book lying open on my chest (a copy of Heidegger's *Sein und Zeit*). He rings the doorbell once, twice (hoping to find the lady of the house in *déshabillé?*). So many adventures in Doreen's suburbia lately! He hears my loud male greeting and slinks around the side path, rather timidly enters through the back garden gate, a heavy wooden affair with huge black hinges and a concealed button which will open it at the slightest pressure.

Eventually, after minor difficulties, he enters and soon has regained enough composure to begin his pitch. Have we been through this before? He stands next to — almost to the very fringe of — the oval rose garden. Nearest him now, lazily beckoning, is a lustrous mob of pure white roses ("Climbing Frau Karl Druschkis"). One dangles perilously close, whispering in his left ear, which he affects not to notice. Recently, only a few weeks ago, the neighbourhood was aroused by a brutal rape-murder. The body of a young housewife was left in — what some would say was an *inexcusable* condition.

He is selling a new product, a device which monitors safety razors and emits a just-audible signal, at a very high pitch, when a dull blade warrants changing. As a "robustly hairy" male, he says, I will appreciate this feature. But he seems not particularly pleased, himself, with the device and is hesitant about permitting me to inspect it more closely. He would *prefer* to show me, at some future date, a product he can support one hundred per cent. Now, my father had been a salesman (before his sudden death by suicide) though markedly unsuccessful at it. And for that matter I was at times a salesman myself, repeating the family folly. Thus I listen to him with an apparent regard which is not entirely his due. Like an ass, he continues to describe, while depreciating, his product.

Since my . . . accident I have been a person whom it is not easy to deal with. Nevertheless, on this unremarkable occasion, my patience and even my deference remain, to the salesman's limited vision, unflawed.

Let me take you back for a moment, I trust not inconsequentially, to the year 1956.

A truck is parked in front of 27 Waratah Street, Brioche-by-the-Sea. It is late in the harvest season. On inspection, it proves that the truck, a flatbed International Harvester with the picket sides in place, is loaded with rockmelons. Perhaps five hundred of them. They are quickly ripening in this furious Briochan autumnal sun, and many are already beginning to rot. A melancholy child is looking at them through the window.

Melancholy? This then would be my kid brother.

We have a new kitten in the house. It is contentedly lapping up its first dinner of cow's milk. It will be several days before it is accidentally killed during our childish games. In the course of a full re-enactment of the film version of Sinbad the Sailor. *I of course will be Sinbad. The more odious role of the Roc — and other minor parts — will be played by my kid brother.*

A man enters wearing a RAAF flight jacket. My father on leave from some war, the first time I can remember seeing him.

My brother and I must sell the melons over the weekend or they will all rot, and my father will be out of pocket. So as to avoid this deplorable follow-on, we fill hessian sacks with eight or nine melons each; then set off in the Saturday sun.

Amy, the girl across the street, opens her door to my knock. It is her role, in our re-enactments of Sinbad, to play a half-naked princess. She does not bother to conceal her amusement. She gives the melons a succession of tiny squeezes before selecting one to her liking. While she runs off to fetch her piggy bank I engage her parents in light conversation. They ask why I am not out playing football, "like the other boys". They have borne the brunt of too many of my sales campaigns: the Christmas cards, the magazine subscriptions, the ear-corn, the bath salts... I reply, stiffly, but as politely as possible, that I am a businessman, that I have gone into partnership with my brother, who is presently working the street on the other side of Old Catfish Creek Road (the poor neighbourhood), that this is the usual division of territory.

So much for 1956.

The salesman is droning on with his soft-sell but the facade concealing my boredom is beginning to crack. I almost wish he were selling vacuum cleaners as I badly need one and have not been able to get out to the shops. It is confusing — the number of options available in vacuum cleaners. I need some guidance, even a demonstration, which will help me come to a decision. Was it vacuum cleaners he professed to be selling last time he was here?

By now I have decisively closed my copy of Heidegger and managed to extricate myself from the hammock. The magnificent sound-system inside the house is flawlessly reproducing a higher-numbered Beethoven symphony. I place myself squarely in front of the salesman, listening as with cocked head while he exhausts the repertory (it is not large) of his assumptions about his product.

The age of micro-electronics has made this product possible for the first time, though, as a virgin effort by a young Melbourne firm, it pales beside some of the *American* achievements in the same genre. On the garden table, for I was meditating after a bit of gardening, lies a pair of sharp, glistening, garden shears — alongside a pretty baroque pruning hook. And sap-stained garden gloves. This all harmonises with the black and white cover of the English translation of Heidegger and the blackish-whitish sounds of Beethoven digitally reproduced.

Belching out of the house, Beethoven!

There is a rosy radiance coming out of the west which now drenches my garden in colour unseen at other times. The rose garden itself begins to glow, the "Frau Karl Druschki" (pure white), even the "Climbing Souvenir de Madame Boulet" (deep yellow-gold) magically transformed. The salesman steps back inadvertently and an "Irene of Denmark" scrapes his neck roguishly. He had a haircut, shave, manicure this morning; so his hand goes up inadvertently to intercept, insult, the rose. It is late in the day now for a salesman to be covering his territory. Before my accident I would have been one of those husbands expected home at any moment, a time for salesmen to vanish.

Trying to keep my voice level, I say: "Have you noticed that children can only sell things on weekends and, as it were, after hours?" He glances about quizzically, his gaze coming to rest on the huge digital clock mounted over the smooth-sliding triple glass doors leading out to my verandah. A thought crosses my mind:

He might be a real salesman.

I have had triple doors installed at the back of my house partly because of my . . . collection and partly as a result of the accident. It makes things so much easier!

The salesman looks disappointed. Disappointed with this last contact, with his day, with the week. Atrocious things have been happening in the mad city of Doreen and he no doubt feels he always misses out on the action, arriving always a little late or departing a little early. Is he taking my comment as a reproach? I was only trying to indicate that, contrary to first impressions, life has a logic of its own. Shall I try to make amends by showing a more than usual interest in his product? I ask a few questions about the Melbourne firm, founded by a pair of enterprising brothers who quit their humdrum jobs and borrowed money to gamble on the elder brother's genius. The product's price has not yet been mentioned.

In sugary tones I ask how much it is selling for.

The salesman apologetically names a price and it seems astonishingly high for such a tiny device. He points out, however, that price need not be, for any product, directly proportionate to size, and that even the inverse might be possible, as witness the case of this product.

"And utility?" I ask, not at all unkindly. The salesman demonstrates, with several examples, that utility and price, as well, are often in inverse proportion.

The current low price of potatoes is cited, with other instances. This is too much!

I walk quickly towards the garden table, seize the mottled sap-stained gloves, pull them on in haste (they never go on fast enough when one is in haste — a thought that comes too late to be of use to me) and pick up the heavy shears, glistening like deer-guts in a summer shower. I turn to him with the long sharp blades sparkling in the evening sun, which glows reddishly now, to each and every living creature an emblem of itself.

"And . . . would the same be true of these, these hideous garden shears? They are very common, *and* very useful, wouldn't you agree? And yet they do not come cheap — on the contrary! Not if they are fashioned by the cunning craftsmen of Doreen.

"What has happened to the old-fashioned notion of *craft*, by the way?"

The salesman takes a sudden step backwards, right into the arms of a "Mrs Suzie Doppelmaier" (velvety white-black, scented) this time. He stumbles over the low border of reddish brick and topples into the "Lavender Ladies" (lavender-blue, high centred). His seersucker coat (always they wear seersucker — or sharkskin — who do they think they are!) catches up on the outcroppings of the luxuriant thorns. He struggles for only a few moments then subsides into them as if now he is at last willing to listen to the antinomies of pure reason. The enigmatic product itself has fallen onto the carefully trimmed turf.

I am a polite man, with a certain physical charm that conceals both my affluence and my scholarly attainments. And yet I too have my breaking point . . . Calming myself I walk over to where the device has landed in the grass, stoop slowly and pick it up, slide it into my blazer pocket, next to my old meerschaum pipe, a legacy from my father. With the baroque pruning hook (which was the only object remaining on the garden table), I carefully sever in half a large banknote, a note worth twice the price of the now negligible product. One half of the note I stuff into the astonished salesman's coat pocket.

As the sun descends disconsolately in the west I make my way towards the sliding glass doors. At a signal from me they open instantly. As I step inside the house, to rejoin my collections, my memories, I turn to the commercial traveller who remains silent, still recumbent, in my rose bushes.

"Tell the two enterprising young brothers, for me, that I am well-pleased to be their first customer!"

I am an accomplished lip-reader, by the way. As I glance out through the heavy glass I can see him now attempting to regain his feet, his composure, his self-importance. His lips forming words which I can readily make out:

"You bloody bastard! You... you can really tell one hell of a story!"

II.
THE BUILDING INSPECTOR'S VISIT

The doorbell rings. It is the Building Inspector's party. With him is the teenage daughter. Her figure is unusually full and shapely for a fifteen year old. She is wearing a two-piece sunsuit, and a bosom urges its way out of the top of the garment.

While the sun shines nothing in the world can be lost utterly.

The Building Inspector's irascibility is legendary. He has been irascible since 1968. After a few muttered words he enters the house, beckoning to his little party to enter quickly. In the foyer is the white telephone I have only recently installed. It has a ten-number memory and a ring-back facility. Sometimes we become over-proud of our gadgets, and yet are they not our only secure possessions, too humble to exercise the imagination of the practised thief?

He is followed by the teenage daughter. She's rather tall... Down, down the monotonous hallway across the fine-grained jarrah floor gleaming as if it could never fade from the gaze of a man with an eye for the texture of life.

Stopping in the middle of the long hallway, the teenager examines her sandal strap. Adjustments are made and the progress of the maiden (as we feel she is) across the jarrah floor continues. I have spent many a night, in our rainy season — to the consternation of neighbouring stickybeaks — with my face hooded, goggled, with heavy ear-protectors, pushing the electric sander over these floors. But that time is past, it recedes into a pinkish memorial haze.

The Chief Building Inspector of the City of Doreen lost his wife several seasons past. She had come over with him from the Old Country. Arriving in our little province, in our largish but hospitable town, she was immediately bewildered by the strange pattern of stars in our heavens. For this we were not responsible, but this signalled the beginning of an irreversible process of deterioration leading to her death at a lyrically early age. Vanishing with her, no doubt, was a considerable knowledge of the country cooking of her native region. In Doreen peasant cooking is held in high esteem.

Since then the Building Inspector has lived alone with his daughter. And since that time he has redoubled his exertions at his trade until he has come to be regarded as one of the best in his field. We see him now take out a handkerchief, a whitish one, with fading monogram, for it is a hot day, even inside this corridor.

Our little party takes a turning in the corridor, and we are now almost in a rush. A bathroom is on the right of the foremost of our now silent band. A bedroom (dark, but not sinisterly so at this hour) is directly ahead. This is the Occupant's room. The corner of the Occupant's bed with its monogrammed covers can be seen by the last few members of the group we are closely following. Shapes can be seen in there — perhaps it is only a curtain blowing in the unseasonable wind which has begun to pick up in the last few minutes. The poor man's only daughter is still having a bit of trouble with that sandal strap, and so she has *fallen a few steps behind* the remainder of the party.

She comes to a halt before the bedroom door. The tall, elegant Host has taken a turn to the left. The foremost man of the little party is expressing doubts about his own state of health. A few medical questions tossed in the way of the Building Inspector are ignored by the latter, as he restores the white handkerchief with a deliberate, graceful (surprisingly so for such a corpulent man as he has become in the last few seasons of mourning) gesture.

Nothing in this world is ever lost or could be lost utterly so long as there is a sun and moon overhead, remarks the foremost of the party as they negotiate the turn into the widening corridor.

A ringing sound is heard in the corridor from behind the foremost of the party, our Host, who immediately turns and retraces his steps. The ringing continues as the Building Inspector comes to a tentative halt. His fat, thick hand fumbles in his trousers.

Leaving the Building Inspector behind him the Host retraces his steps, reaching the door, the foyer, and my white telephone. Both telephone and doorbell are ringing.

Where is she now, the fifteen-year-old virgin?

We call that the Spare Room, says the Host smiling down on her.

Yes that is what we call the Spare Room, he says, his smile broadening in the half light of the corridor here at its narrowest point. The jarrah was polished to a high gloss only the week before by a subtle craftsman. But — beware! — as the girl is beginning to notice, such floors are slippery! As the blushing virgin is beginning to notice. She has not brought the proper shoes, only rough beach sandals. For she has never before accompanied her father on his rounds. This would be the first time.

This would be her first time, she thought.

This would be her first time, he thought.

This would be her first time, he thought, hauling it again out of his trousers.

Slightly soiled, crumpled, wadded up, but still flexible, still usable. A few more years in it yet, this white handkerchief.

A bit stained and stiff but still white-glostered and fine-textured with a softish feel to it in the hand.

This is the sort of handkerchief of which dreams are made, that makes us long for the past and for distant countries where the craftsmen have not yet become corrupt.

One hundred centimetres square, we will not see its like again.

Ever so long ago its mate was lost in the washing machine, in the days when Thelma and Edna still took the crank in hand and squeezed it through until it emerged at the other end, pristine, flat, as if newly truant from a world of filth.

But enough! Or we will make too much of this wonderful object.

The Assistant Building Inspector, a tall serious young man of about twenty, is at the door of the mammoth old residence. He stands beneath the crenellated tower overshadowing the entrance. Only a few seasons past he — also — had come over from some Old Country. He could have remained the Immigrant Who Never Adapted, who kept egotistically to himself, who could not join the community. And yet even this young idealist must earn his crust in this hard new world he finds thrust upon him. The Tenant greets him and then turns to answer the telephone on the marble-textured table top in the ornate foyer.

In the Spare Room I am trying to get some well-deserved rest but rest seems to elude me nowadays, what with the fame, and the attendant responsibility. But I continue to play my part in the jolly dance of circumstance we call our city of Doreen.

Let's have a look in the kitchen.

Taking notes copiously now, the Building Inspector rounds a second turn into a room brightly lit with a huge glass door at the one end giving onto the garden. The garden shows as a furious tangle of greenery. A large urn suns itself next to the fountain.

His turgid notes do not daunt the Building Inspector, whose vigil beside his defunct wife's bed, in what had been their Spare Room, had accustomed him to paying painstaking attention to detail.

Meanwhile, the Host and the Assistant Building Inspector are retracing their steps down the corridor.

"Something fishy in this. I don't like it."

Of course they seldom do like it.

The young man hurries ahead, apparently upset over something the smiling Host has said about the Tenant, perhaps, or the Occupant. Perhaps even the Owner is involved in all this. The young man whom I have sensibly called the Assistant Building Inspector remembers the night before when he had eaten dinner in the farm kitchen with the Chief Building Inspector and his daughter.

They had taken a cup of coffee and the Assistant Building Inspector had leant on the mantel of the fireplace.

That is to say, at the chimney piece of the fireplace.

She was wearing a sensible gown gathered at the bodice and he had gazed down as if *into* the glistening young skin. Her well-developed bosom was not lost on him, as nothing is in this world rightly considered, so long as the sun shines brightly over us all.

Entering the garden the Tenant, the Occupant and the two Building Inspectors move in a group towards the fountain, passing on the way the darkened shade-house with its shifting shapes inside. As of one accord they pause before the fountain. When from behind the fountain appears the Owner accompanied by the Guard. They must have recently quarrelled. Approaching silently the Owner makes a gesture of welcome which they return.

Entering the darkened Spare Room she sees a tall silent figure standing next to the mantelpiece. He is inspecting her boldly, following her slightest movements.

Who are you?

The Assistant Building Inspector questions the Owner about the premises. The Building Inspector has withdrawn his extracts and, still consulting them, drops heavily into the chair.

A Robert Manwaring chair is rusticating near the fountain.

I said who *are* you, he says.

She turns around quickly, and the strap falls off her shoulder. Her bosom . . .

Enough is enough.

But by now she is well into the room and the figure has drawn very near to her. And *something from the bed* begins to heave towards her as well . . .

But now the Guard has to have his say:

''Nobody can be lost utterly — even in an indifferent universe like ours. Crying out to be humanised by our own presence.''

Whew! Does this mean that nothing is going to happen to her after all?

''Humanised by our own *passions,* don't you mean?'' interjects the Host.

Oh dear, does that mean she might still be in *trouble*?

The air is hard to breathe, foul, used up, as if the chamber were crowded with invisible beings who had not supped on human flesh for a long, long time.

So Maureen, the Building Inspector's Daughter, decides to step outside.

Quite correct. The simplest solution to a threatening situation.

The Chief Building Inspector resumes doing what he was doing before. So do the others, including the Host himself.

III.

THE BANK MANAGER'S DAUGHTER

Dear Dr Vladich,   23 December, 1986

I would like to take this opportunity to extend to you compliments of the season! You would, I am sure, agree that 1986 was an eventful year, particularly in banking circles.

As foreshadowed at my last time of writing, the Bank of Doreen has undergone substantial development over the last few minutes. I would like to draw your attention to the recently introduced extended range of accessible accounts. If you have not already done so, as your bank manager I strongly urge you to take advantage of these facilities — immediately.

As mentioned previously, a new service fee is being introduced — in fact is already in effect for those who selected our "Option Account" prior to five seconds ago.

ETCETERA YOU RICH ODDBALL BUGGER WHY I CAN STILL BUY AND SELL YOU.

Speaking as your manager, and I trust for the other employees of the Bank of Doreen, including the willowy "girls" at the counter, I look forward to your continued patronage and wish you well for next year, which I trust is 1987.

ETCETERA ETCETERA SIGN IT FOR ME WILL YOU AMY?

Yours sincerely,
T. K. A. Mockingbird
Branch Manager
Bank of Doreen

At *precisely* nine o'clock the bank manager arrives at the Doreen bank branch. In fact this is the place where I do my banking. He is *my* bank manager and not an empty fiction.

He has just dropped off his sprightly teenage daughter. She is a student at Doreen High, once the most exclusive school in our stuffy little metropolis. Once. For scholarships have brought a common, roughneck element into the school. From the country, from Port Doreen.

She has well-shaped breasts, full for such a young girl. The night before she had been reprimanded for spending too much time on the telephone. The bank manager, to his credit, is considering presenting her with a personal telephone for her sixteenth birthday. I fervently hope so. But he is of two minds about this. Her breasts are full, well-shaped, but also of two minds.

While his teenage daughter jauntily mounts the endless steps of the high school, the bank manager pauses, idling his Porsche, preparing to dart off to the city to face acute responsibilities. He takes a last thoughtful look at her. From a distance she looks like a fully mature woman — not his own daughter. In fact she looks like just the sort of woman my bank manager might fancy if he were not happily married to a rather skinny horse-fancying woman from an old Doreen family.

At precisely nine o'clock he enters his inner office, punctual as always — a man of habit.

He is dressed . . . well . . . conservatively. The tie is bold but this is a lively branch office. It is in the centre of this unpredictable city, but still a backwater, overshadowed by the main branch only a block away. There is very little meaningful communication between the main office and the branch where I prefer to bank.

In my years as a client I've been treated well by the branch office.

The bank manager's daughter decides to stop in the toilet to have a last check in the mirror. Admiring herself in profile. She notes with pleasure that it is *all still there*. Why do we put ridiculous sexual constraints upon the young?

Somewhere in the inner sanctum of the bank a telephone rings. As the branch does not open to the public for another hour, nobody answers the telephone, which continues to ring incessantly as if to sound the depths of the bank manager's considerable holiday hangover. (I in fact am urgently trying to reach him about the new Option Account. Also I need a loan, quite a bit of money in a hurry.)

His tie a very bright red, the telephone a sensible white. Then the ugly but efficient secretary enters the office. Later the attractive scatterbrain will enter, asking him if he "needs anything" today.

She is pretty, scatterbrained and young, quite young — as time has not yet begun to erode her looks — and she still believes in men.

At about ten o'clock I step down from my bus. I have been delayed this morning, since a wildcat strike temporarily disrupted transport.

I can't say much for the transport system of this city of the plain, perched as it is on the far edge of the civilised world, lying supine, heat-stunned, below the greenish hills I love to motor up into. And yet my researches require that I ride the bus every day. (My Maserati stays locked in the garage until the evening.)

As I step down I scrutinise my fellow passengers. "The drivers ought to be given the lash, publicly castrated and then, after watching their genitals being fed to the dogs, summarily shot," I quip to the attractive housewife who has disembarked just in front of me, her timid daughter holding her hand. The mother is ready for a day of airconditioned Christmas shopping. She's dressed to the nines, clutching her tiny purse. And she trusts the day to bring whatever it must.

All in all this is a commendable attitude and she is not visibly offended at the sly sexual innuendo in my speech. I am a stranger to her, after all, with all the privileges this conveys.

The Deceased File, a compendious document, because many people have in the past died in this sun-blasted city, is placed silently on the bank manager's desk. He looks up at the girl intently, casting a quizzical and yet seemingly bored glance at her, at the roundness of her arms, so visible in her fresh white garment.

For the time being he ignores the Deceased File. Head bowed over his work — or so it appears to the admiring secretaries who, from time to time, glance over in the direction of his cubicle, the inner office. But he is really thinking of her.

On the way to her second class of the morning, his daughter stops at her locker to fetch her Life Problems textbook — for at week's end there will be an exam and she is ill-prepared. In fact her marks have been slipping steadily throughout the term. She has her mind on other things. Behind her two boys give low whistles, which she pretends not to hear. One of them, Ratso, is a few years older and has a bad reputation. It is said that he once killed a man, a farmer who had come after him with a shotgun for interfering with his thirteen-year-old daughter. The farmer's own shotgun had evidently been turned upon him. Shortly thereafter the girl herself vanished, as so many teenagers from our odd little city seem to do.

I make my way down the Doreen Mall towards my bank branch. Passing the chocolate shop, I see the plump Angela in starched white frock behind the counter, but she does not see me. Just as well, as it is too early in the morning for a sample of hysterics. Last weekend I stood her up. But then I had not expected the Hard Mart girl to accept my bantering invitation quite so readily. There was no time to ring the chocolate shop. Besides, according to my calendar, Angela would have been *hors de combat* for that particular evening.

Things are not flowing smoothly at the bank branch this morning. Colleen Green, the newest girl, a mere trainee, and thus totally without rights among the other counter clerks, had to be put in her place by Amy. It seems the old Professor Emeritus had come in, asking for his weekly allowance of ten crisp twenty dollar notes, and had been asked to wait until Colleen Green confirmed that he was a depositor. The professor had reeked so of cheap wine and — something else, rather goatish — that she doubted he was a client of their branch.

And then his dirty fingernails had been drawn across her little tortoise-shell bracelet!

Just when Amy has finished putting Colleen Green in her place, the door to the bank glides open and I enter. All heads turn towards me (I do make an impression with my dress and demeanour, not to mention my singular physical characteristics) and Colleen Green is dispatched towards the empty counter which I will cross over to, once I have paid my respects to the bank manager. He, at a word from the ugly but efficient secretary, starts up — waking from some unspeakable dream — and walks over to the door of the inner office from whence he greets me cordially.

In fact I can tell he hates my guts.

I decide I will not ask him for that loan this morning. But I'll open an Option Account at the least. I can put off some of my more expensive adventures for a few days.

I see his hunched shoulders as he withdraws into the inner office. He is not a well man today. A pity!

Nor is his high-breasted fine-boned daughter. Between classes she runs for the female toilets, enters the nearest cubicle and hastily examines herself. Yes, on time — what a relief!

As she leaves the toilets, she can hear a couple of boys sniggering behind her back.

— Is she the one you mean?

After providing a specimen signature for the flustered Colleen Green, I boldly look up to meet her eyes and then, while she is puzzling over my cryptic handwriting, I unleash my goatish gaze and allow it to snaffle down her neck, down, down (a dizzying, cisalpine trajectory). Such are the everyday violations that go along with being Human. I allow the ash to fall off my cigarette onto her skin, since for just this instant I am feeling quite the Nazi inquisitor. But she dusts it off her hand, absently, her mind somewhere else. She is in a snit over her work, worried about getting it right. This is the first Option Account she has ever handled.

And this is her first time with me!

Just over my head is a sign: NO SMOKING.

After her noon class he is waiting there in his battered van. Ratso is so short his shaved, dented head barely tops the steering wheel. He is wearing a slit and scuffed black leather jacket. At first she pretends not to see him. His van is next to a sign: NO STANDING.

— Hey do you want a ride?

All too soon it is closing time. The bank manager takes up his flat black briefcase, fills it with papers, several of them relating to my estate (on a tiny offshore island in this district) and moves through the hiss of the sliding glass door. Colleen Green stands at the door to the bank, watching her new boss depart.

There is something about that tired slouch of his that suggests defeat. Today is just not his day. Things can only improve in the year to come. It refreshes him to think that at least he has his daughter, the only reason he thinks his life is worth living! Tomorrow, hangover gone, he will doubtless change his mind.

Colleen Green walks back and forth in front of the bank window, the Automated Teller that is threatening her new job. Her feet are killing her. She walks a little way up the pavement, but, as if tethered by an invisible skein, she does not move away from the Automated Teller except to return as quickly as she had left it. Then she tries immobility, but this, since her feet are killing her, is also unsatisfactory as a posture of expectation. She stands and stands, growing more and more impatient.

I am watching her from a phone box opposite the bank. Just when she decides to stop waiting and walk off towards her own probably dingy flat, I step up quickly to her side, offering my apologies. Now she is almost pitifully grateful: not stood up after all. She taking my arm (the good one, the left one, the one left), we cross over the street and head for the Carpark Tower.

We are only two people riding in an open Maserati. We might just as well be two drunks hailing a taxi. At the light, I give way to an insistent Porsche, just as we are overtaken on the inside by a — *battered panel van* — that appears unoccupied.

Why is she working at this particular branch, where the chances of promotion are so incredibly — like her ankles — slim?

I ask her this question in the Maid and Magpie — a little cellar pub which I have, over the years, made my special hideaway. It is such a fine and private place that, in all the years I have been coming here, I have never seen another customer. And yet Sam the Barman is always there to mix my special drink and Jan the Barmaid, too, is always on duty, always at my beck and call, only too willing to cater to a regular customer's whims.

Well, well . . . it so happens that Colleen Green used to be the bank manager's daughter's chum, when they were at summer camp. She filled the part of big sister to her, since she was always getting into scrapes. Colleen had saved her from several close calls with boys, so . . .

So as usual it was a question of influence. The main office would not have hired such an inexperienced person, but the branch manager did so. But the other girls at the branch, who do not even know these facts about her, have made life difficult. They have even broadly hinted that she is "following" the bank manager. Or that he, usually beyond reproach in his treatment of employees, especially fancies *her*! A tear glistens in the corner of a large candid blue eye, round and perfect. I offer to dab it with my handkerchief, a monogrammed silken affair which I am afraid is neither very clean nor very absorbent, but which she accepts with a show of gratitude.

Later, waking up in my enormous silky bed in my townhouse bedroom, I admire, for what seems now the thousandth time, the ripeness, the nakedness of my Colleen Green. Lively images of our night together replay themselves before my eyes, like remembrances of first things, the beauty of a newly created world where only I — or we — can roam in the presence of benign tutelary gods and tiny furry animalkins.

Awake now, in this night city of dangerous visions, I am oddly mindful of old Sir Isaac Newton and his curious *fluxions,* which were just his way of clarifying (without *dispelling*) the universal darkness.

The girl's eyes opening just then. *The rate at which a variable (flowing quantity, fluent) increases or decreases at a given instant of time!*

Ah, but then it is with a kind of sudden sorrow — the sorrow of a vast plain of waving pampas-grass in the midst of which rears up a ruined alabaster citadel, inscribed with petroglyphs I shall never decipher — that I remember her:

The bank manager's daughter!

IV.
THE PILOT

Level by level, as from a fountain spilling into some walled-up courtyard of the mind.

The girl said they were selling tickets for the Doreen High lottery.

The boy said, "That's right."

Doreen. Pop. 1 100 000. Main imports: electronic equipment, spirits. Main exports: whitegoods, wines.

A bag of groceries was sitting on the verandah. The boy and the girl looked at it. The man in the doorway was clinking the ice in his glass of scotch. The radio was on, in some inner room, playing rock music. He must have left it on, turned up loud, when he had gone out to the shops.

Standing in the doorway he took a long drink of scotch while they watched.

"Would you like a drink?" he said.

"Sure, why not?" the boy said.

"It's okay with me," she said.

He led them into the lounge. Then poured out two half-tumblers of scotch, added ice and a splash of water. The boy handed one to the girl. The man poured himself another.

"Down the hatch!" he said.

They knew the house well. They lived in the neighbourhood and in past months had sometimes entered it when nobody was home, just to fool around. This man was either moving in or moving out, they couldn't tell which. Some rooms didn't have furniture. There was an echo to them.

"I'm a pilot," the man said.

The boy and the girl sat side by side on a sofa-bed in the lounge. The man brought the groceries in from outdoors and, returning, handed each of them a second tumbler of scotch.

"Down the hatch!" the man said.

The boy once found a woman in this room. It was a hot afternoon and he had broken in just to get out of the sun, hoping to keep away from his parents for a few hours before tea time. He did not see her until he had helped himself to a beer from the fridge. She was still in her nightdress. Despite her resistance he did what he wanted to do.

Now the girl was starting to lose control of speech. The man seemed unaffected by what he was drinking.

"Mind if . . . okay if I kick off my shoes?" she said.

"I am a pilot," he said.

The girl got up and walked barefoot through some of the empty rooms. In the study she found the radio and turned it up louder.

She looked at some photographs on the shelves. A pretty almond-eyed young woman faced the camera boldly. Two girls in school uniform. A handsome middle-aged woman.

The man brought another shopping bag into the lounge. There were more bottles of scotch in it. Potato chips, cheese dip, cabana sausages.

Then he topped up their tumblers.

"Down the hatch!" he said.

The girl's fingers carelessly drummed on her knees. The skin was almost transparent, showing the fragile bone at the shin. By now it was late afternoon and through the picture window they could see a green back garden filling up with blacker shades. There was a tiered white fountain out there, the bright water spilling down level to level. All at once a piping shrike swerved towards the window, a commotion of wings, then peeled out of sight.

The boy moved to a black leather chair placed in a commanding position in front of the TV, which was turned on with no sound. The test pattern was on. The set was tilted at an odd angle to the wall, so that from the command-seat the lead-wires were visible.

"So you really are a pilot," the girl said, stretching out on the sofa-bed, then drawing her knees up carelessly. Her voice drawled off absently.

"What do you fly?" the boy asked without interest. He too was growing lethargic.

"Women," the man said, "I like to fly women."

He was ripping open a bag of potato chips.

Later the boy dragged himself out of the leather chair and stumbled over to the sofa-bed. But he ran into a large dry cactus plant as he went, the needles catching him through his thin shirt. The girl could hardly move as the boy squeezed in next to her.

"We better get going," the boy said, his speech slurred.

The Pilot said nothing.

He poured himself another drink and then walked over and put a video cassette into a machine under the TV. He watched it for a while, drinking more scotch. He did not look at the boy and the girl, who were beginning to doze off on the sofa-bed, side by side.

The boy's arm was wound around the girl's torso.

The Pilot settled down in the big leather control seat in front of the video. He played several cassettes in succession:

A. This tape was simply a recording of a boy and a girl lying together on a sofa-bed.

B. This tape transcribed the same — or perhaps a similar — boy, but this boy was with a woman. His image was crouching over hers as it lay on the floor. Its enormous bright eyes were frozen on a subject, or point, just behind the camera.

C. This tape was totally blank. The Pilot played it several times through, on fast-search, forward and reverse.

They looked as if they were sound asleep, the pair, the boy and the girl.

He finished a tumbler of scotch and then stood up.

"Down the hatch," the Pilot said.

V.

THE LIFEGUARD'S VIGILANCE
....

At nine in the morning, at one of Doreen's southern beaches, the lifeguard arrives for some agile surfing before he begins work. He has been stationed here for some three years, quite a spell in our province. Successful lifeguards usually head for the bigtime: Catalina, Balboa, Coney Island. For the first two years his mother drove him to the beach each day. Then he started appearing in his own vehicle, a dilapidated panel van. I haven't seen his mother since then. The life of a lifeguard's mother probably would not bear looking into.

It was also a year ago that our beach murder transpired. The lifeguard had coolly loitered about the girl's corpse, as if it were just another drowning victim. Murder was not his province. In our province murder is the province of the police. In our province, in the South, accident — drowning — prevails among the young. Hence the lifeguard.

Today he sits erect, but a trifle moodily, up on his tower, five ladder rungs of aluminium above the rest of us. He rubs his monkish shaven head thoughtfully. He is in point of fact rather small, wizened even, but not from this angle, as he towers above us all. At the base of this structure an attractively structured woman has been spreading out her towel carefully — for the past three years — so as not to trap too much sand, and has lain for the most part with her bum upwards, her head towards the water. Up on his tower the lifeguard reviews his thoughts of the day insofar as this is consonant with his duties — which are not onerous for most of the year except during Doreen school holidays when extra vigilance is demanded.

When you get youngsters at the beach you have a recipe for trouble.

So why do I insist on appearing at the beach in my ludicrous beach gear when all around me the kids are looking for trouble? Well, for one thing, I like to see how the lifeguard handles himself. The kids look up to him but they frequently put his authority to the test, and it is precisely at these moments that I draw as near as I can to the tower, in my feathery, ganderform beach costume, approaching from the dune side rather than the beach side.

From this position I can observe precisely the point at which authority transforms itself from amiable toleration to repressive violence. This point is a variable one in most areas of behaviour but it is even more so in beach-life which has (as a rule) its own rules.

She rolls over on her towel every half hour or so and it is then that her firm belly and . . . well, everything else, her other piquancies, are displayed to the skies. Besides the lifeguard and a pervert or two farther up the dune and an occasional hang-gliding enthusiast, few observers can really get a good angle on her.

As the lifeguard reviews his thoughts of the day he also keeps his moody eyes keenly on his work, his watery horizon.

He has had perhaps a poor morning of surfing, no suitable waves. But this would not ordinarily be enough to trouble him. No more than would a highly motivated crime like murder. He is only interested in unmotivated behaviour: accidents.

Once each year the regulars of the beach throw a barbecue and the lifeguard is given his annual present. In the past it has always been my duty, a pleasurable one, to present the award. With a little speechifying. I have discovered one cannot be too ornate or too inconsequential for the quaint folk of Doreen.

The annual present is always the same, an embossed beach towel-set with the crest of our smallish city emblazoned on it:

DOREEN
CITY OF LIGHT.

Sand is a relentless element. Every year it takes its toll on our synthetic fabrics, the weaving of which is our main industry. She turns over on her stomach again and the buttocks wriggle slightly. As she adjusts her book.

She is reading a novel by and about a woman who was born in the outback, came to the city for her education, married, was deserted by her husband (after having lost an only child to an obscure nervous disorder) but eventually became...

The day of the other young woman's murder I had come earlier than usual to the beach. Instead of arriving alone I was accompanied by my overseas visitor, Claude. He had wrapped up his year's work at the Sorbonne and so had come to have a look at our folkways. And if there was time, he would glance at our *mores* as well. By her repeated turnings she has managed to collect on her gleaming ripe flesh quite a number of sparkling grains of very fine white sand!

But surely murder is not one of our folkways nor is it one of our *mores*! It is true that the Bank Manager's daughter was found in an inexcusable condition not so long ago. And it is also the case that the Building Inspector's daughter did not fare well at the hands of an unknown badperson. And it is furthermore correct that the girl at the Kentucky Fried outlet (the daughter of the Franchisee) met a nasty end, as did the General Magazine Merchant's daughter, who vanished while collecting for her paper round.

So it goes in our city of Doreen.

I was afraid Claude might get the wrong idea.

Later, in answering the polite questions of the mustachioed young policeman, Claude's unflappable manner proved most helpful.

Particularly to me, as I was asked — absurd as it might sound — to explain my own "whereabouts" that morning and the night before. As Claude and I had spent a riotous evening drinking and spouting exhausted European philosophies (existentialism, satanism, structuralism, postmodernism) to the patrons of The Tower of Rats Charmed by Music (my unique local pub) — an alibi, like one of our local synthetic fabrics, was quickly spun up.

And now she decides to warm yet another aspect of her anatomy: the...uh...slim haunches have not been receiving their due. Elaborately, she applies her Golden Goddess cream (sun factor of two). An expensive formula! She has just now reached the end of her second tube of it this summer. Otherwise, summer is cheap for this sleek creature. Semi-retired, her career in prostitution now behind her, she owns a prosperous little boutique and a charming villa in a decent suburb of our city. Born a publican's daughter, she occasionally thinks of her ailing father, whom she visits every day in the Doreen Hostel for Incurables.

The shapely corpse had been wearing a T-shirt with LIFE. BE IN IT printed on the front. This struck Claude as a delicious piece of "found irony". His tattered notebook was out quickly, his Bic flashing in the sharp rays cast by thick spectacles.

Thus I could savour Claude's gratitude for my invitation to Doreen.

Now she at last gets up. Has she had enough sun for today, then?

Drawing her TODAY IS THE FIRST DAY OF THE REST OF YOUR LIFE T-shirt on over what Claude once decribed as her *râtelier splendide,* she pauses only to glance up (squinting in the sun) at the lifeguard. He acknowledges her homage briefly, knowingly, then returns to scanning the horizon for exclusively accidental disasters. A hang-glider hovers overhead, surreal, as if suspended in a devil's radioactive amber.

As she threads her way gingerly through the scorching, infernal sands, I too decide I have had enough sun for the day. Gathering my feathers up around my midriff, I farewell the lifeguard in the customary way, a modified form of the old "Rap" Brown black-power salute.

As usual, he ignores me.

How weary I am of it all!

With a sigh, I too set out — awkwardly, owing to my inflatable rubber footwear — towards the carpark area. My intention being gradually to close the distance between us, so as to arrive at the carpark precisely when she nestles into her tattered Volkswagen.

A few half-naked schoolchildren run past me, hooting and screeching, as if the sight of a man wearing a duck costume were an excuse for commotion.

TURN LEFT AT THE
NEXT TACO STAND

Maybe each of us has a way of taking unfair advantage. At least Alabama Red had.

"No more tricks, Conchita! You're not going to sell your sweet ass any more. On or off the street. Right?"

The education of Conchita was taking more time than he thought.

"Look, I need the money, I need the publicity. Maybe even I need the self-respect."

"From ten million guys slapping you up on their bathroom walls? Or — thinking of *you* every time they sink their cavities into a Taco El Rancho Grande Deluxe?"

Alabama Red always won eventually. He had a knack for moving along oblique lines, slanting into his relations with other people, so that the sense of reality — of a shared reality — was immediately at risk. He could take advantage of this because he was used to it and the other person, the target person, was not. He was a left-handed tennis player, too, and the advantage was the same. Only at the top of the game do you meet other left-handers. Down among the amateurs, the percentage of left-handers is about point-one-five.

Alabama Red noticed one summer's day with a sense of shock that

135

the world is run by left-handers, who were playing the only game in town.

Conchita was smart and she was a very beautiful kid, but a left-hander she was not. She was straight and honest as a glass of branch water. He said to himself: that's the con, the puritanical dream, to make it the honest way, hard work. That's making it on your *back,* baby!

But when Conchita told him she had decided to enter the Taco Queen contest, he eventually said sure that was okay. He even helped her fill out the entry form. In fact — because she was too shy to go along and be seen as "prospective queen" — he spent one whole afternoon driving around LA looking for the places where the entry blanks were supposed to be available. "At all Taco Queen outlets", the advert had said. But every outlet he went to they were fresh out of forms. It looked like every little scuzz in LA was entering the contest.

Finally at a little off-the-main-drag Taco Queen, a dingy, seedy one that looked closed when he drove up to it, he found an old guy behind what appeared to be a vomit-stained counter. The guy reeking of stale sweat and El Cheapo tokay. On the wall behind him Alabama Red saw a pop art poster: a coronetted cowgirl coyly straddling a giant taco.

> ### "If God Didn't Want Man to Eat Tacos
> ### He Wouldn't Have Made Them Look Like They Do!"
> ### NO CREDIT
> ### — Charlie Sympathy, Prop.

This Charlie Sympathy — who probably lost his franchise about the same time he lost his teeth and hair — somehow knew that Alabama Red had not come in to buy a Taco El Rancho Grande Deluxe. Nothing was cooking on the grill, anyway. Not a taco in sight. The proprietor of this joint was picking his nose with his *left hand,* a skilful man.

Fashion note: Alabama Red was wearing his new black leather Ike jacket, tie-dyed cotton shirt, purple Dynamesh Slaxx, and Glo-Soxx.

He bought this oufit when he heard that UCLA was giving its professors a pay rise. Alabama Red was the recently appointed Jerry Lewis Professor of Popular Culture.

"So you know somebody wants to enter the contest? Listen, schmuck, those so-called contests are setups. Keep Etta Mae back on the farm. You wouldn't want all those meatballs out there in consumerland to pop their cookies over *your* lady?"

"Come on, *pops,* when I need advice I'll ask my shrink." (He had wanted to use that line for a long time.) "Pops" was so old maybe he's Death Valley Scotty. "If you got forms, just give me forms."

"You're a nice polite kid. I'd hate to see you get hurt is all. I should tear up these forms. How many you want?"

Every Tuesday-Thursday-Saturday afternoon comes Tiny Voice Time — Conscience Searching Hour. Introspection: driving back along the Santa Ana Freeway, Alabama Red could meet himself coming and going. He was thinking about Conchita.

What would winning do to Conchita? Anything worse than losing?

Alabama Red was an introspective type, of Puritan stock. ("When you see a Puritan coming you should cross to the other side of the street," Kierkegaard had once whispered to his mistress.)

Maybe this contest would work to his advantage, putting Conchita in her place once and for all.

As has been noted, in the area of human relationships Alabama Red never played equals as equals but stayed among amateurs: for instance a woman racked-up from a divorce is an amateur. And so are most pretty young women like Conchita.

Conchita apparently had nothing to trade on except her youth, and so Alabama Red insinuated that youth was just not enough. He affected to hold her youth against her. He would chastise her for her youth and scold her for her good looks. This particular number had never been tried on her before; she had been an arrogant beauty, thinking (too right!) that every adult male in LA wanted to get his meathooks into her. Alabama Red's stratagem deprived her of her foothold on common sense.

From then on Alabama Red, who could sometimes be a shit, handled the Conchita situation from a position of strength. Most of the time.

Conchita had had an uneventful youth. She had fallen for a twenty-eight-year-old hustler when she was fifteen, still a San Quentin quail. She had liked Stevie's fast car and his devil-may-care approach to Life.

Predictably enough, within a few months Stevie had her on the street supporting one or more of his sordid and dangerous habits. But the pain of it was in discovering, one hot smoggy afternoon, that she was only one of his many girls. She had thought she was . . . a contender.

Not much later (as He must for us all, but usually not so violently), the Iceman Came for Stevie Starkweather . . . The charred remains of his heavily modified Mustang were found in Laurel Canyon, violating the anti-litter laws on about two thousand counts.

At the LA County Morgue, Conchita could identify him only by the moodstone ring she had once given him. The liver-pale colour of the ring — usually a pulsating purple — showed that, just now, Stevie was in no mood at all.

Alone now at eighteen, Conchita stayed on the streets, her heart no longer in her work. Deciding eventually to upgrade herself she enrolled at UCLA for a few classes in urban planning and architecture. That's what most of the smart girls were doing. The streetwalkers would build the City of the Future. And why not Conchita? Her College Entrance Examination score had gone over the top.

Alabama Red had first met her at Tower of Records on Westwood Boulevard. He had cruised by on his way to a seminar he was giving that afternoon on "The Doris Day Syndrome". He was trying to score a fresh copy of the Doris Day Classics (1954) album. Then he noticed someone lingering around the Dean Martin bin. (Which was where Conchita usually scored her Dirty Old Man pickups.) She was wearing thick vermilion Max Factor eye-shadow, pulsating glo-yellow halter-top, and Frederick's of Hollywood hotpants.

They were fire-engine-red hotpants.

Alabama Red that day had the randy throbbing species of hangover he called the Oestrogen Special — where he found he was capable of approaching pram-pushing mothers, grocery-bagged housewives, bike-riding teenagers, in the streets, in the shops, on the beaches, at the cinema, you name it. They never knew what to make of him. But there was a high capitulation rate. The pheromones really hit the fan when he had that hangover. He would prowl the Nowhere City, feeling horny as an Arab in a hijacked airliner.

"Look, Conchita, you got to sign the forms yourself, and they want a recent picture — in a bathing suit."

So they went off to Corona del Mar for a swim that afternoon. She took her two-pieces-of-string job. When she changed on the beach, the divine Conchita nearly caused a riot among the pathological skateboard and unicycle set. Somebody had once offered Alabama Red a German shepherd attack dog as a gift. But he was above taking bribes just for approving somebody's MA thesis. Now he wished he had accepted.

So the Jerry Lewis Professor of Popular Culture got his girlfriend to writhe on the beach, in suitably suggestive attitudes, for an old Leica, while erectile juvenile delinquents and a couple of older, tougher guys stood around, in casual-menace poses, indifferently leafing through their tattoos (octopi entwined around skulls, dripping eyeballs) with switch-blades. Everything those guys wore was black, which (remembering Psychology I) suggested to Alabama Red a negative social image. But he himself was wearing black leather...

Fortunately a couple of topless sand bunnies came along just then, distracting the hard guys, who have a short attention span.

Alabama Red took the film over to Harvey Hotchkiss at the

Westwood Image Mart for instant developing. Harvey, who was an old peace movement buddy from the Vietnam days, would keep a few of the negatives for himself. That's the kind of guy who gets into photography — or as Harvey called it, perhaps misleadingly, "the film industry".

A week after Alabama Red sent in the application envelope, Conchita received the following letter:

Dear Taco Queen Aspirant

We at Taco Kingdom note with concern that Mankind's most intimate relationships are too often grounded in idle opportunism instead of Transcendent Reality. And as Immanuel Kant used to say, what higher Reality than Taste itself? And what Taste more sublime than Beauty as found in the Human Female? And, to compare great things with small, what tastier and healthier than the Taco?

We are clued-in enough (while not being wise-guys) to understand that while there are no Ethical Absolutes there still remain certain constants, however hot and savoury, in Life *per se.*

And female exploitation is just another way of perpetuating the living evil that is everywhere symbolised by the promiscuous growth of fried chicken outlets. Not to mention the ubiquitous hot dog and hamburger.

The hamburger is only a taco designed by a committee. A committee of male chauvinist gringos. As for the hot dog —

We at Taco Kingdom believe that the anodyne for evil lies in Diet and Compassion, both of which are literally and figuratively bodied forth in the taco. As Groucho Marx once said, form should always follow function. Nature's most perfect form, the sine wave or parabola, inheres in Nature's most functional food, a food beloved of millions of the world's peasants and labourers while remaining the favourite of kings. Verily, Perfection itself is taco-form.

If you can relate to the Taco Kingdom Philosophy, we invite YOU to get your act together and come for your Profile Interview at *9 p.m., Friday, April 23.* The address is Taco Kingdom, 66666 Wilshire Blvd. Come alone, bringing evidence of your age. Use Security Access Code No. *558-770.*

(Signed)

Victor Mature Tostada

Director, World Promotions

The Taco Kingdom is a five-storey oblate spheroid of a building that looks like a flying saucer from below, a football from the side, and a tortilla from the air. It has no windows. As in the Pentagon, its antitype on the East Coast, the higher echelons of power are housed in the upper storeys. Which means, folks, that architecture reproduces social structure.

Conchita looked at the buttons in the lift. Top Floor: HRH Tomaso M. Fabilla, King Taco (Access Forbidden). Fourth Floor: V. M. Tostada World Promotions (Key-in Security Code for Access).

She typed her code number into the keyboard and waited. The lift rose swiftly. The last thing she remembered was a piped-in recording of Peggy Lee singing "You Played Around with My Love..."

Six months later, Conchita was crowned Taco Queen for the Twentieth Century. The press conference and reception was held in the Grand Reception Hall of Taco Kingdom. The Jerry Lewis Professor of Popular Culture (flanked at the back of the room by a cluster of his favourite students) stared intently at the reconstructed image of his own Conchita. The transformation was total, from head to toe, left to right, back to front. While feeling a touch of the pride of a creator in his creature, Alabama Red did not loiter there (next to the champagne fountain, glass in hand) with unmixed feelings. As a team of photographers and reporters from the LA *Mirror-Times* pressed forward, eager to close with her, Alabama Red thought he could guess the cost of his protégée's sudden elevation.

For a tall, latin-looking man stood silently at Conchita's side. Victor Mature Tostada no doubt had a certain role to play in the elevation of Conchita. The dark, handsome man listened suavely, deferentially, as she outlined to the press her plans for the total urban renewal of LA and went a bit into the philosophy of Buckminster Fuller, whose singular notions of architecture were embodied — updated appropriately — in the design of the Taco Kingdom. She added that the Taco Kingdom's shadowy ruler, King Taco — HRH Tomaso M. Fabilla — would make a rare personal appearance on this very occasion. His own paternal interest in the Queen-elect was confirmed by all the Hollywood rumour-mongers.

Alabama Red lingered at the edge of the reception, occasionally dipping his hand into a tray of smoked oysters *en tortilla croûte* or chili *relleno quiche.* He did not expect that Conchita would acknowledge his presence at such a moment of triumph for herself. But he was curious about what the evening would bring. Some of his students, mostly those who were into media and marketing, were keen to have a gander at King Taco himself. And they were enjoying a brand of champagne that students — even at UCLA — rarely get a chance to taste. It was a special Rothschild bottling with the Taco Kingdom seal on its label.

There was a fanfare at the front of the hall and the heavy damask curtains parted. The lights went up on the previously darkened stage and an eldritch electric hum was heard, a buzzing sound as of an approaching mobile beehive.

A figure in a thronelike electric wheelchair powered into sight, describing helix-like circles, as if madly out of control on the smooth marble surface of the platform. After careening a few times around the stately motionless figure of the Queen, it stopped finally at her side.

So this was Tomaso M. Fabilla!

King Taco raised his sceptre — in his left hand, Alabama Red noticed — as his mysterious countenance glowed, taking the full light of the podium.

"What the heck!" Alabama Red said aloud.

Then, flush with the sense of recognition, he heard himself — his voice was raised involuntarily. And he was almost shouting:

"Charlie Sympathy! So you were Tomaso M. Fabilla all along! That means — hey!" Alabama Red's mind was moving with the speed of light, now: that foul-smelling little taco shop probably had had the *only* entry blanks in the Greater Los Angeles area. And thus it was likely that Conchita was the *only* girl to enter the Quest!

"Justify this imposture, Charlie — if you can! And I speak not as a private citizen, mind you, but as the Jerry Lewis Professor of Popular Culture!"

Heavy hands — Taco Kingdom henchpersons do not pussyfoot around — were laid on him, and somebody was just about to hand Alabama Red his own *cojones*, or worse, when King Taco began to speak.

Silent orders were given and Alabama Red found himself momentarily free.

The weary voice of the Taco King seemed to come from some great polar — or stellar — distance. It did not seem to make a lot of sense at first. There were spewings of exhausted European philosophy and Eastern wisdom salted with copybook truisms. The yonic significance of the taco was somewhat dubiously related to the double helix, to the notion of infolded and reduplicated universes: the visible universe of the banal everyday reality, and the "Universe in Reverse" where right is left and wrong is right. Where male is female and beggar is king.

Tomaso M. Fabilla levelled his gaze at one person only in the crowded hall:

"And so," his voice croaked, "my learned challenger will appreciate that this entire exercise has been to teach him a much-needed lesson about Life. An elaborate lesson, and an expensive one. He was giving off bad vibes, real bad karma, and making life generally unpleasant for one helluva fine woman. Let us hope he has learned his lesson well!''

"And what *is* the lesson, pray tell?'' This was the voice of one of Alabama Red's loyalest students, no doubt hoping to save her professor the embarrassment of confessing his ignorance.

"Yes, what *is* it you speak of, old man?'' another student rejoined.

At this point King Taco, who was about to summon up a reply, was silenced by a stately gesture from Conchita. The old man subsided into his electric wheelchair, his voice tapering off into a barely audible croak.

The Taco Queen swept the room with her haughty glance.

(Alabama Red now veritably cowering at the back of the hall.)

And then, raising her left hand, the Taco Queen fixed her gaze on her past lover, her one-time reality-instructor.

"The King's voice has passed over to me,'' she intoned huskily. "He will say no more.''

The dark, almost serpentine form of Victor Mature Tostada could be seen at the rear of the stage, swiftly propelling Tomaso M. Fabilla (alias Charlie Sympathy) into the shadows.

Conchita ignored their silent departure. Her gaze did not waver.

"Now the Jerry Lewis Professor will come forward, to join me at my side.''

Alabama Red paused. What the...?

"Pronto!''

Alabama Red did as she commanded. His gaping students fell back to make way for him as he groped his way towards the dais. The Queen said, in a rich, assured voice:

"A one-time king among men, Tomaso M. Fabilla teaches us that the lacework-traceries of the brain, the circuit-loop of the Santa Ana freeway, and the infolded skein of the taco all embody the true form of the Future.

"The mirroring realms of academia and free enterprise, long

thought to be merely unrelated, today will proclaim their deep and abiding affinities and unfold their shared objective!

"We can't — uh — go into the *details* here, of course, but rest assured that together, academia and free enterprise, of which the Jerry Lewis Professor of Popular Culture and the Taco Queen are but the outward and visible representatives, will build a new LA, which truly will be a new — City of the Angels!"

The crowd of newsmen, students, FBI agents and Mafiosi began applauding wildly as the royal pair bowed to their homage.

Alabama Red was not too sure he was up to it, but maybe it was worth a try...

LITTLE BOY LOST IN THE LIMESTONE CITY OF MY HEART

For as long as they had been together Tom and Becky had been planning an expedition to the caves, but for various reasons it had never come off. That night — after a few drinks — he proposed it again. Time for something new. They had not been getting along well for some months. One of their bones of contention was whether they should have a kid. Tom felt he had already had his share some time ago. Becky, younger than Tom, childless up to now, claimed to want a little boy in Tom's image. Tom regarded this as a biogenetic form of idolatry.

Okay — they would drive to the far south-east of the city of Doreen and spend the night at a favourite last resort of theirs — Green Mansions. The next morning they would drive the additional half hour through the hills to the limestone region.

"In zee limestone zere ist zee freedom," he said, twirling an imaginary Pancho Villa moustache.

He could be very amusing at times.

There were three caves. If they got an early enough start they would be able to do them all in the single afternoon.

As they drove up to the entrance of Green Mansions, Frances was already on the verandah, in an exaggerated attitude of expectation. Tom and Becky were demanding guests, she knew. Unlike most of the other regulars they were not escaping from kids. They were in pursuit of that precise level of distracting luxury which would keep their hands off one another's throats.

Frances caused their larger bag to be carried up to the Blue Room, but a smaller one Tom kept to himself. The bottle of malt whisky was in the smaller bag. He would wake up at three or so in the morning and tiptoe to the upstairs library and read maybe a volume of Raymond's poetry, sipping scotch until he felt sleepy again. Later, if Becky were thrashing about in her sleep, he might wake her and she might accept his lovemaking — if managed quickly and quietly. And only if no . . . uh . . . *precautions* were taken.

Tom saw that the only other guests, an elderly man and his young wife, were occupying his favourite spot in the drawing room — in the little alcove where they could gaze out over an inviting expanse of garden. From late afternoon until the call for tea, the man (a doctor, it turned out) and his wife languished there, murmuring conspiratorially in the fading light. Frances and a girl from the kitchen were minding their baby, a cherubic boy-child, who was trotted in from time to time to be petted by the doctor and then suckled noisily and conspicuously by the roseate young mother.

Thus Tom was reduced to prowling around the perimeter of the garden (Becky bored, napping in the Blue Room). He observed, ruefully, that the doctor's Jaguar was already parked just where he himself liked to park his toy, his dream, his (heavily mortgaged) Porsche.

Later, Tom let the good doctor taste his displeasure by indifferently acknowledging Frances' introductions. The doctor, blissfully ensconced, did not register the pique, though he affected to be sorry to miss the chance of buying Tom and "the girl" a drink. Tom also made a point of not acknowledging the existence of their Infant Phenomenon.

The next morning, Tom overheard doctor and wife misbehaving in the shower together, the woman giggling and snirting outrageously. (Becky, still sleeping like the dead, was doubtless totally unaware of Tom's nocturnal overtures.) It seems Raymond's poems had not sufficed for the early hours,

> holding to the book like a wheel,
> sweating, fooling my life away...

but after consulting several heavy scotches, Tom had managed to get one or two extra hours of shuteye.

He was a bit sluggish coming down to breakfast. At quarter past nine, when he did manage to creep forth (with Becky in tow, dishevelled, still at least partly comatose), it was a deeply apologetic Frances who explained that they might wish to take breakfast out in the unseasonable chill of the terrace. The cosy little breakfast nook had already been bespoke by —

"Don't tell me — the doctor!"

"How did you guess?"

There are certain horizontally extended caves under hills whose rainfall never could have provided the ground-water flow needed for their creation. Such caves must then be more ancient than the hills and valleys of the region. The ground plan of these caves suggests the street-system of a city, a multitude of narrow, linear, intersecting passages.

An underground city, Tom thought, putting aside the pamphlet. A sister-city to Doreen, then. But dark, ancient. Far older even than the plain beneath the hills, on which, unaware of this archetype, Colonel Light had caused the latter city to be erected. Foursquare Doreen, city of Light. And this other dark city, *a city prior to men!*

Like almost everything in Australia the caves would doubtless not prove as spectacular as one might wish. The tour of the largest cave was destined to cover a full hour, but its tourable regions were greatly reduced, closed down when Mines Department inspectors found that recent earth movements had loosened tonnes of soft limestone.

So the success of the tour would hinge on the guide's ability to inflame the imagination of the visitors, most of whom, on the present occasion, were locals from surrounding hamlets and farms, with their principal children. Two pneumatic Amazons, classic schoolteachers-from-the-east syndrome, Tom thought — obviously hellbent on touristic sin — were part of the group too. Finally, the doctor and wife, who clung to the guide of the day — named something like Bodkin or Botchkiss.

When, in his deep, cultured voice, the doctor murmured comments or questions — about the marsupial fossils for which the cave was renowned — everybody listened approvingly.

Tom had not been into a cave since the days of his first marriage when he and his friends — all married too young, all trying to escape wives and kids — had regularly gone "spelunking" in the High Sierras of California. On these expeditions, Tom, Ken, and of course Raymond, would drive Tom's rusted, expiring Chevy up into Amador County late at night. The existence of "Black Chasm", as they called it, was unknown to the public at large. They would conceal the Chevy in the manzanita and carry their equipment the mile or so to the entrance. They took standard mountain climbing gear plus carbide lamps — and scuba-diving tanks for the underground lakes.

According to legend Black Chasm had once been the hideout of Joaquin Murieta and his gang of banditti, who, during the days of the Gold Rush, were notorious for robbing Wells Fargo coaches and disappearing silently into mountain fastnesses before the *Federales* could find their own saddles.

If they had used the cave, Murieta and his boys would have been a formidable gang, since entrance can only be gained by a twenty-foot downward rope-climb (and eventually you have to climb back *up* again), followed by two hundred feet of rappel down a vertical shaft. Then the climber reaches a four-inch ledge, situated another two hundred feet or so above a crystalline subterranean lake. After sidling along this ledge for a dozen yards one reaches the base of a vertical pipe, a chimney in the rock, which can be negotiated only by bracing both feet against the opposite wall and shrugging upwards for about *twenty* feet. A slip of the foot in this slimy, dripping chimney will lead to monumental discomfort, since it evacuates directly into the sunken lake far below.

But after climbing the chimney, which takes a gut-wrenching half-hour of twisting about like a spitted viper, you draw yourself up through the floor of a magnificent limestone chamber! Under the beam of a carbide lamp, it gleams with unearthly reflections. Here you see virgin rock formations of all types: stalactites, stalagmites, halectites and long delicate "straws" (like hollow stalactites, eighty feet long). The floors of this vast chamber — which Tom's friends named the "Crystal Cavern" — are washed by swift channelled rills of gin-clear water which falls in silent sheets to the lake so far below.

This probably inspired Raymond's lines:

suddenly I find a new path
to the waterfall...

Tom and friends would spend days exploring underground, often probing in total darkness to save fuel and batteries. The only signs of human presence were evidently created by themselves on earlier forays: minute disturbances of delicate mineral formations. Or *was* this their own spoor? A trail of ruptured stalagmites...or a boot-print in a soft spring-bed...

Caves can cause disorientation, dangerous visions, even madness. Tom and his friends suffered re-entry problems: re-entry into the real world of work, marriage and child-rearing. Black Chasm caused three teenage divorces. Boys will be boys. Boys will, evidently, remain boys.

Once, only once, in all those visits, did they find — or believe they found — testimony to other human presence in the caves. Near an airshaft, perhaps miles from the entrance, Raymond reported having seen a single word written in candle soot: FUEGO.

Old Bodkin or Botchkiss had started out as a cave guide in the thirties. He was newly married then and the caves were as virgin as his wife, he said. (Snorts — from the schoolteachers.) Then he had gone away to the war. Returning several years later he was astonished at what people had done to the caves. Desecrations had been committed below ground surpassing those of the war itself.

"Look here — this stalactite used to join up with the stalagmite on the floor, but somebody broke it off. A hundred million years in the making, too! If I ever get my hands on the culprit the punishment will fit the crime."

A tiny fair-haired boy stands near the guide at the front of the column of tourists. His parents have — evidently — lagged behind a bit, leaving their son a hostage to pedagogy. The guide glowers at him as if he were the guilty party.

"But now take a look at these things over here, these things that the girls will say look like something naughty. What do you see, young ladies? *Eh?*"

At almost every twist of the passageway, the guide's amorous belly squeezes one or the other of the *sportif* Amazons up against the chilly limestone walls.

"I've been into parts of these caves that nobody knows about. Gone there with girls, sometimes... There's no harm in an old married bloke still having at least an eye for a pretty lass, is there, eh?"

Tom, involuntarily turning, cannot immediately locate Becky.

"But look here at our main attraction — we just recently discovered this fossil over here, after a landslide. It apparently is a giant koala — petrified! Along with one of its young, like it is hugging it. They are over a hundred thousand years old. A few weeks ago I took a crippled girl down here. That little girl just had to see that koala. She said she would never get another chance..."

So I carried her down here on my back. Light as a feather. That koala brought tears to her eyes.''

Tom is peering off down the side passageways now.

Has Becky just fallen behind the rest?

The little boy is fidgeting near the grasp of the guide.

''Can you tell us how these fossils got here, then?'' The doctor's mellifluous question.

''Well sir, I reckon one fine day, thousands of years ago, dozens of wallabies and koalas were probably having lunch together — just over our present heads, that is. Then the ground — which to get technical was a base of calcareous rock hollowed out by the carbon dioxide in the water flowing through — just caved in all of a sudden — and swallowed them whole. And they remained buried here until Sam Forsythe discovered this cavern in 1967.

''Sam Forsythe mainly found the bones of some little joeys — but by then they had turned to stone.

''Just like you'd want to happen to your mother-in-law, eh?''

Complicit giggle from the Amazons.

''So this would be one of the more important *finds* . . . ?'' (The doctor speaking.)

''Yes, sir, but how many people know about it? Cave guides are not supposed to get political, and I won't, but nobody, not politicians nor those young radical schoolteachers want to talk about the real Australia, about the true Down Under — down under in these caves!''

For emphasis perhaps he gives the boy a pretty rough shoulder-shaking. (No parents in sight?)

''Well, getting back to you, young ladies — these naughty looking things are called *halectites* and nobody knows why they stick out the way they do.

''My personal theory is that they are just mutants. You know, just like every family has its normal children and then every so often — nobody knows why — one kid out of every half dozen or so is born a . . . not to mince words . . . a *freak*.''

He gives the boy a wink. Tom notices for the first time that one of the boy's shoes has a complicated brace attached to it, and a built-up sole.

"It's as if Mother Nature wants to keep her failed experiments — her *freaks* — underground, in the dark. And if you think about it, that's maybe where they all belong!"

It appears now that they are coming to the end of the safe part of the cave.

"Has anybody here ever been in the dark, before — the *real* dark? I don't mean dark like when you get up at night to try to find the dunny. Like I do two or three times a night."

Predictable snickering from the schoolteachers.

"This little lad here is afraid of the dark — aren't you?"

Another shake for the boy. The boy nods, embarrassed.

"And he has an idea of what it would be like if he got stranded here — *alone* in the dark, doesn't he?

"I'm the only person here who knows his way around this cave in the dark."

Tom remembers Black Chasm when the carbide ran out. They had spent twenty-four hours in the dark. The "real" dark. Raymond had written:

> You wake, look for the sun in your face,
> But you don't remember,
> You really can't remember . . .

Suddenly — predictably, Tom thinks — the cave floodlights go out.

The schoolteachers, only a step or two ahead of him, give happy little shrieks.

Now where would Becky be?

And what is old Bodkin or Botchkiss up to in the dark? Evidently no sound from him.

You can't tell time in the dark. It seems five minutes pass. The lights stay out for rather longer than a joke.

In the midst of sounds of whispering and scuffling Tom neither speaks nor tries to deflect an enquiring hand that moves down from his shoulder to his thigh. But then another hand — a different person's? — finds him in the dark, touching him less tentatively...

"Mummy, when will they turn the lights on again — I'm scared!"

"Hush, dear, somebody's just playing a joke. It's hide and seek, but don't run away! Mandy, where *are* you? Stop doing that to your mother, dear! It's not nice to poke people!"

"Heyyy... watch it, mister!" An excited girlish voice.

"Somebody's got me too!

"Makes no difference who, in the dark, does it?"

"Help! It's the Giant Koala! Arghhh! Arghhh!"

"Stop it, Edna, or you'll get us in trouble when the lights go on!"

Tom remains silent, listening. He can't tell if a hand still lingers on his body. If so, it remains quite still, content where it is. He stays frozen.

Scuffling. Suppressed squeals. And — an echo — maybe from deeper within the cave. A dull hard repeating sound. And, nearer, a harsh, rough breathing.

And then, farther away, something like a bark.

Probably just some slavering beast out there prowling around, Tom thinks. Maybe coming this way, from some distant chamber of the cave, hellbent on mischief and wanting a little white meat...

But what the hell *is* going on?

"Where's the guide?" A man's voice raised now, agitated.

"Maybe he's gone home to find the wife."

"Or maybe *your* wife!"

Suddenly there is a new sound — a kind of gargling gasp.

And — then a sharp outcry.

It hangs there as an echo for a moment.

Hurried stumbling footsteps...

From below . . . a sound like a boulder falling into water. And then a slipping and splashing — like a small avalanche of rock into water. Not a cave-in?

What did the pamphlet say?

The circulation occurs chiefly along the horizontal bedding planes and the more commonly vertical joint cracks, the water moving under gravity to lower levels and eventually to escape as springs and seepages. The sides of these primitive passages are attacked — especially in the presence of carbon dioxide (as from animal respiration) — and thus enlargement results.

Animal respiration? You mean — us?

The lights go back on.

For a few seconds everyone is blinded by the light.

Looking around at the scattered file of explorers, Tom notes that almost everyone made the mistake of wandering about after the lights went out.

And that would appear to include Becky, too. So where might she be?

One schoolteacher, grinning at Tom, nudges her friend. (That's the one as done me, Edna.)

Just then Becky touches Tom's elbow . . . having slipped up behind him. She is shaking like a leaf.

There's no sign of any injured party, but the cry — uninflected as to sex or age — sounded genuine. Everyone looks around, feeling for their wallets, handbags, children.

Is anybody missing? How would anybody know? You don't sign anything when you buy a ticket. (Best to come down with a friend.)

Bodkin or Botchkiss's clothes looking rather a blotchy mess.

"Okay, everybody!" Breathing heavily, the guide is adjusting his tie.

"Okay, everybody! No worries! Every time, just before we leave these caves, I turn out the lights for a few seconds.

"But this time somebody . . . somebody must have moved the switch, eh! Is everybody okay?

"Makes you think, makes you really stop and ponder, doesn't it? Where would we be without good old Light? In the dark is where! Our whole species is afraid of the dark. That's why we are always burning up fossils. Need fuel to keep the lights on around the clock."

The doctor is murmuring to his wife. She seems quite shaken.

Bodkin or Botchkiss mounts some nearby stairs they hadn't noticed before. They lead to what appears to be a hatch on the ceiling of the cavern.

"Those poor little stoned joeys were down here in pitch dark for thousands of years before Sam Forsythe came along. But with all those fellows — upstairs — playing around with uranium...

"Causing trouble... Just to keep the Night Light burning... When it does happen, then all the lights go out anyway. And who will be around to let the light in on *us* ever again?"

"The Giant Koala!" somebody sings out.

Fossils from seventy-eight different species, from frogs to a marsupial about the size of a bull, have been found in this cave. As for other unfossilised mammalian remains...

Such as — folks like us? That would be interesting to know.

Becky is holding Tom's arm more tightly.

"Let's never have a baby," she whispers. "Something might go...wrong with him."

"*Him?* Anyway, *that's* no argument, that's not even a reason," Tom says, surprising himself.

Becky looks at him with a rather odd expression.

They are all pressing forward, eager to get above ground again. Children are getting fidgety about toilets and food.

"Darkness is a great equaliser," Bodkin or Botchkiss says, his hand still fiddling with the bolted hatch. "In the dark everybody is as good as everybody else. Rich, poor, old, young, boy, girl.

"But sooner or later we'll all end up playing fossils together in the dark.

"See you then!" He unseals the hatch.

On the way back to Green Mansions they have the Porsche's sun roof open, just to let the wind blow on them a bit. Up ahead, the doctor and wife have outdistanced them in their Jaguar. Becky lays her hand on Tom's thigh.

Resting there on his thigh, his lover's hand seems to him weightless as a distant bird — just another floating scrap of matter detached from fields of gravity they are now transecting, at this particular time of sunset, in their silver machine.

After prolonged silence, Becky turns her face to him. He can feel her eyes. Maybe she is looking him over, appraising him once again.

"Tom?"

"Yes, luv?"

"You didn't just happen to see that little boy when we left the cave — did you?"

"Didn't notice. Maybe he belongs to old Bodkin or Botchkiss."

"Or . . . ?"

"Or what?"

"Or maybe we had better turn around."

KRAFFT-EBING NOTES:
···

No. 206: A BIZARRE CASE OF SEDUCTION ATTEMPTED IN A FOREIGN TONGUE ABOARD A SEAGOING VESSEL

Call me Bogart, Sylvester Bogart, if you want to. That is not my name, however. I sailed to the USA from Europe early in the year 19—, and this is my story.

I had managed, without a cent in my pocket — by means of an innocent stratagem — to secure cabin-passage aboard a Holland-America Lines freighter from Rotterdam to Houston, but the Indonesian troubles required that the Dutch ship disgorge its passengers in New Orleans, instead. The *Zuiderkruis* was needed in Indonesia at once to take prisoners from one island to another island. An unfortunate change of course, as we spent three days in a hurricane in the Gulf of Mexico. This was the mischievous Hurricane Annie-Zelda Rasmussen, which we had picked up just after passing the Isle of St Alonso and it fronted us all the way to the Georgia Sea Islands. During Annie-Zelda Rasmussen I learned how to doze off on bulkhead walls and to swallow egg soup while upside down in a marine toilet.

At this period, however, I derived a small comfort from the fact that Elmo Crappanzano the chief steward was as ill as I was — iller, actually — and was thus prevented from protracting his amours with a certain pneumatic German divorcee.

For had I not spent most of the voyage trying to attract the attention of this Ulrika — whose favours I had craved ever since my belated and rather compromised arrival on shipboard?

In all there were only twelve official passengers (I was the thirteenth, a last-minute, "unlucky" addition) and we were closeted together in a special compound. Since I was a young, unattached male (thus, a "student") — the only such among the passengers — and she was an extremely flirtatious and erotically inflamed female, I might be pardoned for thinking the chances of my success with her were "assured", as they say in *romans du boudoir*.

Note that I had been reading far too many *romans du boudoir* in my roach-ridden Barcelona *penzione*. There was nothing else I could do since I was a penniless traveller and was thus unable to pursue any of the Spanish *vixens* I could spy passing in the streets below. And yet I fancied these women to be in a state of perpetual excitement corresponding to my own, and thus aching for lovers of any description.

Ulrika was travelling to Houston to the arms of her fiancé (a Texas oil millionaire) and the merger was planned for a few weeks after disembarking. I was travelling back to California to join my own fiancée, Lena ("Legs") Lowenthal — president, Kappa Alpha Theta sorority — but we had no immediate plans. Ulrika and I thus had a little in common. I had also spent a year in her own country. As a hitch-hiker: no money and lots of needs.

"Seduction", if it ever was truly possible, is no longer fashionable, so I'm tempted to draw a curtain on the scenes of attempted seduction on the boat. But the God of Truth is a stern and exacting taskmaster. As a nineteen-year-old American male, of course, I could not employ all the armoury of the practised seducer on a sophisticated European woman a decade older than myself. Probably my major blunder was in trying to conduct the manoeuvres

— what were meant to be the preliminaries — in her own language. By so doing I inadvertently yielded vast steppes and tundras to my rival — the oily Crappanzano, chief steward.

Young men are (blessedly!) unaware of how little their youthful physiques and vitality count in the sexual arena, which is a zone — if truth be told — not of bodies but of words and gestures, of social signs and tokens. "Performance" means one thing to a hot-blooded young man who, in the absence of a sexual partner, must shamefully practise the English vice to preserve sanity — and it means something entirely different in the arena of intersexuality, where the meaning of the term "performance" is closer to — dramaturgy.*

And this was where chief steward Crappanzano excelled. The entire repertoire of deferential gesture was at his disposal, along with a fluent command of several languages, including Body. In retrospect, after a lifetime of conducting amours in the most difficult circumstances and with some of the most unlikely partners, I now see that the subtle steward made more headway with the affections of my dear Ulrika, just by silently arranging her napkin on her lap at dinner-time, than I made with my entire array of tactics. Well, two tactics. On one front, Language; and on the other, Silence.

Two devices I employed in irregular alternation: the first was to display my talent for *Spasserei* in her language (a sample of such "jesting" in a moment). The second was to display my large round melancholy eyes, with which I would gaze in meditative fashion at her across the room. This was supposed to convey the impression that I was harbouring the most profound desire for her. A desire...beyond mere speech.

Melancholy equals "poetic soul" equals Lord Byron equals — *fucking*.

I was too naive to know that, instead of displaying how racked-up I was supposed to be over her, I ought to have been finding ways

---

* Note: The Contessa Scorpia d'Amato, among other women to whom I have shown this paragraph, says it is so much bullfeathers, and merely serves to illustrate not my youthful, but rather my mature, delusions about women and the *erotic*.

of racking her up over me. I was parading the *symptoms* of a condition which could be of little interest (unless grossly ludicrous) to anyone who was not herself *already* envenomed with a reciprocal all-consuming passion.

In all of this, I had darkly divined that poetry could be a weapon of seduction — that being vaguely poetic was as good as being an operatic tenor or a football halfback. And since poets do occasionally have to do more than merely gaze (like mute Byrons) they must prove themselves in the agility, *the athleticism of their speech.* All of which would serve — as metaphor? — for the athleticism of the...Disciple of the Erotic!

Now the only regular chance I ever got to engage the target-person in conversation was at the dinner table. All the passengers were obliged to sit at the same table and I had so managed it customarily to sit directly opposite Ulrika. This was the necessary preliminary, I thought, for my onslaught of Wit.

It appeared, from my pocket German dictionary, that there were two ways, in that murky language, to talk about *eating.* One was to speak about the way *human beings* eat — for that one used the verb "essen" ("to eat"). The other word was applied apparently only to the animal world: "fressen" ("to eat, gorge, of animal", the dictionary stated laconically).

One day, as we were taking our places around the table, I managed as usual to fix Ulrika with my basilisk gaze. Once I was sure of her attention I remarked that on this occasion I was so *hungrig* (hungry) that I felt more like *fressen* today than *essen.* That is, I felt more like "gorging" myself as an animal would than eating in a more anthropomorphic fashion. (The sea is a *well-known stimulant* to appetite, ho ho ho...)

The whole truth of a language is not always to be found in the shorter official dictionaries. She had begun listening to me with that strained politeness she preserved during most of our conversations. (I attributed this to her fear of losing control of her emotions; her deep shame at betraying how strongly she was attracted to me.) As soon as my sentence was out, though, punctuated by what must have appeared as a self-congratulatory little smirk ("see how famously I am getting on with my German!"), my listener's face suddenly changed.

Up to that moment, the little group of passengers had been chattering merrily, boisterously, as if ignoring us. But just then a leaden silence fell and all eyes were bulging inquisitively in our direction.

My divine Ulrika's refined expression changed, and a look of total disgust — or was it violent repulsion? — passed over it, darkening (as I then noticed — why had I not noticed before?) this German Frau's heavily powdered, gaudily made-up face. Lapsing into an almost guttural English, she veritably *spat* out the next few sentences:

"Do not — *ever* — say such a thing in my presence! It is too — it is too — *disgusting!* Ooff! Ughh!"

She quickly diverted her attention to the other gaping passengers at the table and ignored me for the rest of the evening. After that, whenever I crossed her path she would avert her eyes.

From that moment the ascendancy of the serpentine chief steward Crappanzano became pronounced.

I never learned any more German. But I have often wondered what was so offensive in my suggestion that I would like to "gobble" my food for a change. I have often since imagined hideous *doubles entendres* couched in my little speech — or nuances of which I was unaware. Maybe I got a wrong gender on a pronoun or something else in there — I just don't know.

I do know that from then on I would encounter the chief steward, at all the odd hours of the night, as he slithered to and from the cabin of a certain shameless, betrothed woman.

And, if I paused (as I frequently did) to listen outside her cabin, I could hear them —

Ulrika's throaty squeals undercut by the low growl, the *basso ostinato* of chief steward Elmo Crappanzano.

Argh! Argh! Argh!
Fressen! Fressen! Fressen!

BLIND PANDA EATS AGAIN

Pandas are difficult creatures. But Pandora can imagine the perfect one. This beast would mate enthusiastically in captivity, bear multiple healthy offspring and never go on a hunger strike. The world's newspapers would lose a few centimetres of copy per week. There would be a saving in trees.

She sits at the little table in her farm kitchen, drawing reflectively on her slim churchwarden pipe. A cat — Ghostbuster — circling her leg.

But pandas are not the problem. People are the problem! People mainly of the male persuasion. She went to veterinary school deliberately to beard males in their own foul dens. But in cornering and mastering the Beast, she feared something awful — akin to the Patty Hearst Syndrome — had happened. Had she not perhaps grown very like the maw-crammed brute she had despised, then humiliated? Well, she sometimes craves...uh...Balkan Sobranie pipe tobacco, coarse-cut!

Poor carbuncular Teddy is one of those males whom females think they should like. His deportment, like his clothing, casual; the rest — conversation, lovemaking — similar. He is pale, reasonably clean and speaks three languages, including Quechua, which is understood only by headhunters up the Amazon. But, alas, none of them is the language of love! Tedious Teddy will bring along a (digital) recording of, say, *The Magic Flute* (sexist opera), and sit there complacently listening, arms folded, leg up on her table...

But tediousness is Teddy's true aim. When in form, Teddy does not cruise down the main highway to a woman's heart; he rattles off onto an overgrown side road, left off the county maps for years. Bumping along in his jalopy of love, he will somehow (fifty per cent of the time) end up where all paths meet.

What to do with the likes of Teddy?

Well, to begin with, have a cup of tea. Pandora's kitchen is at the rear of her surgery. When she's not menaced by such as Teddy, it's a private place (feet up on the table and a cup of tea — sloshed through the servery window by Black Bart, her nurse).

She is nearing thirty, asymptotically. (Asymptote: "Line that approaches, but does not meet, a given point.") Like so many sisters of like vintage she enrols in enrichment courses at the university. But after an ill-advised fling with an unsavoury professor of literature, "Kit" Carson Boone (American, of course), she confines herself to ecology studies.

A ferny orchidaceous garden of her own planting shimmers in the sun that now batters her kitchen window. She pauses in mid-thought, critically: I'm not still "building character" am I? The year in Mexico had built her character. She had been a locum for a Mexican vet, Victor Mature Tostada, and had helped him officiate at the *corrida*. And the year before, in Lancashire, she had built her character during the lambing season, camping for weeks with Dorian Stonecypher and other rough country men. *Lancashire* had been no picnic. But Dorian had had strong, capable hands... The *corrida* had been horrible. An amorous matador had offered her the part of the bull he was in life doubtless most proud of. So Mexico was no picnic either.

It is a fine blue Saturday, no more clients expected. Pandora could abandon the surgery for a long lunch at the Honeypot — a courtyard restaurant in the wine country, but — Teddy would want to tag along.

And the manager, Ernie Baer, an old friend of hers (three years ago they had met on the flight from Singapore), would react to all that was epicene in Teddy, and the wine cellar would suddenly disgorge nothing but tannic, resinous, heavy-oak, brownish, expired, not-so-dry reds. And Pandora liked her wines — and everything else — clean, light and fresh.

No — better to take Teddy to lunch someplace fairly neutral, like the little bistro (Pooh's-in-the-Wood) run by an old Glasgow classmate. (He had failed his veterinary exams.) Rory's surgeon's hands — so capable, she well knew — were devoted nowadays to boning chicken and chopping onions, tears streaming from his long-lashed eyes, down his sensitive face, off his fine-cleft symmetrical chin, into the chicken marengo. Rory proves kind but too attentive. He prowls in circles, refilling their glasses, offering the full measure of the wine-cellar his restaurant is renowned for. But he spills some of the Penfolds St Henri on her Mexican striped dress. Then makes a dumb-show extravaganza of cleaning it off for her.

"If you go down in the woods today,
You'd better go in disguise"
(Pandora humming to herself).

Later, after she has chucked Teddy out (groping, tipsy, snivelling) and is back in her kitchen, feet up, pipe lit, kettle singing on the hob, Ghostbuster trying by dint of paw to make a space on her lap, she contemplates her next half century. She supposes there will be humans involved in it in some capacity — what a pity!

Sunday morning she is out there amongst her tree-ferns, misting them over, soaking their trunks, bracing them up to meet the day. It will be *hot*. She is wearing her darkest, hardest-looking sunglasses. It will take courage for everything to survive this day. She glides about offering moral support to the topocosm she herself has wheedled and goaded into being. The half-dozen resident pussies (watched ruefully from little cages by visiting convalescent dittoes) are stalking one another, while self-righteous parrots scold from the lillipilli tree. Occasionally, when she overturns a slug, there is a beating of wings, an invisible rush of air — and a shred of glistening slug-flesh vanishes into the skies.

The surgery bell rings. On Sunday! This had better be a real emergency. Or maybe it will just be Ursula, her best friend, with the surgery down on the beach road. Ursula will be wanting a cup of coffee (black, two sugars). Leaving her garden Pandora sheds her straw sombrero on the kitchen table, lights the kettle as she passes through.

The person at the door, with a great dog in tow, is Kojack . . . "Blind" Kojack. She has never met him officially, though at the North Doreen supermarket, when he stumbled into a canned pet food display, she (as medical person) had silently helped him right himself, had found his cane for him, had steered him on his way. The cane was certainly an unusual piece of workmanship.

"Blind in one eye and can't see out of the other," he had said to her friend Ursula on their single (abortive) picnic together. She had found him "unbearable", hungry for sympathy.

He was until recently a lecturer on human brain chemistry. Then — something happened. In Acapulco, where he was to be the keynote speaker at an international conference ("Artificial Intelligence: The Medical Implications"), he dropped out of sight for over a week. He was discovered (blind, babbling) in a louse-infested bed in a provincial hospital, all identity cards missing.

Now on a disability pension, Humphrey Kojack devotes his time to research into "the mystery of life". Nobody really knows what this entails. Occasionally a cleaning woman will quit his employ and try to smear outrageous tales around the suburbs of Doreen. But since the employees of Blind Kojack are inevitably disreputable, nobody heeds their mutterings.

So Pandora must open her surgery door to this person. It seems

Barabbas has been indisposed lately with a mild gastritis and there are a few chronic complaints to see to as well. Pandora points out, not politely (she is impatient with human handicaps), that chronic matters should be seen to during the week, not after-hours. Barabbas has cataracts but also an increasing deafness. Not much can be done, anyway. Pandora suggests more exercise, and a careful diet. "Often, if the...uh...master is overweight, the dog will be, too," she says, pointedly.

"Result of the foulest debauchery."

"Pardon?"

"Picnics, mostly — bloody champagne and chicken picnics. I am afraid you see a dog here (poking Barabbas's ribs as punctuation) — a dog who's spoilt himself beyond a hope in hell of redemption. And don't look so proud of it either, Barabbas! You would repel even your own master if you had not made him an accomplice in your...ugh, choke gasp...unspeakable..."

— Choke gasp arghhh arghhh! (What Kojack doubtless means to be a complicit chuckle sounds more like dirty-old-man's chronic emphysema.)

"You give this animal alcoholic beverages?"

"Oh no! — *champagne!* Barabbas will have his champagne and spatchcock and there's no preventing him. Cut off Barabbas's drink, doctor, cut off Barabbas's cakes and ale — and you might as well cut off his..."

Pandora has to shut him up.

"Well, sir, this little *contretemps* today will cost you fifty dollars — cash. Today is Sunday and you've come in without a real emergency, haven't you? That's twice what I usually charge for real emergencies."

Pandora's   because-I-am-virtuous-there-shall-be-no-more-cakes-and-ale voice.

"And cut down on fatty foods — he doesn't need that much meat. Try cereal dog-biscuits."

"You know, I hope you will forgive my saying this — on my

presuming upon our past acquaintance in the...uh...supermarket, but..."

So he actually could see her then! What a *bastard* he was! She had been dressed in a flannel shirt and a ragged pair of jeans.

"Well? What? I don't really have any more time for you today, sir."

"But in these few brief encounters...I have grown to trust you, to...*like* you, as well."

"Nonsense!"

"Your style — like when you ask for my money. Ah...Doctor! I think I am falling into the preliminary stages of *caring*. For a veterinarian! A word I can't even spell!"

Pandora is ready to send him packing.

Maybe.

"Wait! Look here...*doctor!* If you would take off those dark hard sunglasses and let your hair down, you would be...you might be... But then I can't see you anyway, of course. Do you take the usual credit cards?"

"Cash, I said!"

"Doctor!"

"Yes?"

"What are you doing for lunch?"

They lurch up in front of the Honeypot in Pandora's Orsino Ghia Turbo. As usual she slams into the kerb in order to stop. Barabbas with sleek old head slobbering out of the sunroof. Kojack, tall, heavy, extricates himself with a sea-captain's grace from her car and, after a few melodramatic pitches over small obstacles on the footpath, manages to secure her arm in a vice-grip. Pandora does not see how she can make him let go, since otherwise he keeps heading with a kind of death-wish for bushes, light poles, passing traffic. He leans on her with an exaggerated heaviness, as if he has suddenly become a paraplegic.

"This little encounter..." he gasps in her ear with his hot breath, ''reminds me of a book I wrote once about the human brain. Brain-chemistry teaches us...uh...well, whatever the specifics were I forget. My brain must be Out to Lunch, so to speak.

''Wait! I do remember something I found out. Like how the neurological structures operate as constants in human *culture* and that modifications in the former cause changes in the latter.''

''Nonsense! Worse than nonsense — blather!''

''No — trust me! It appears that electrical patterns in the brain behave like the plots of stories we have read over and over. Do you see my drift? We are enacting a story which has *already been written* in the very molecules of our brains. And so of course we already know the conclusion. Congratulations on our pending engagement!''

Great! Just great! Ernie Baer overhears this, with a show of wry mirth. So from one point of view the lunch is not a success. If there were a wine-country in Hoboken or Banff or Tierra del Fuego, the wine that Ernie dredges from his cellar would have to represent its most shameful vintage year. Pandora, however, notices a change in her internal weather. Er...a kind of feeling (highly qualified, riddled with conditionals) for Old Kojack.

She must *care*. Otherwise (for she had warily stipulated that lunch be her treat), why does she turn a deaf ear to his blubbering request for champagne and chicken in heavy cream and mushroom sauce and instead order him cottage cheese and crudités with Ryvita? (Stipulating, for herself, a juicy fillet steak.) As for the wretched Barabbas, she directs Ernie to find him a handful of hard dry dog biscuit — to be served outside!

Relationships, especially those between highly educated men and women, undergo vicissitudes that can be plotted on a time-axis. Most of these are so commonplace that they do not bear looking into at length. Teddy of the Carbuncles was demoted to cognomen ''Theodore'' and forbidden access to the surgery except for bona fide emergencies involving his sickly show-hamster colony. Ursula was of course consulted regularly on all aspects of dealings with the male race. Her advice was succinct: dumping the dubious Teddy was an admirable step. But consistency demanded that Pandora jettison Kojack, too, before things "got worse".

But Kojack kept on coming around. It seemed Barabbas was having trouble with his digestion. The old mutt was failing to thrive on the new, healthy regimen, however much Pandora insisted and persevered. She showed Kojack her old Glasgow textbooks.

Kojack sniffed at the publication date of *Canine Nutrition* (1952).

Could it be that Pandora was not keeping up? No, she knew her job.

But then one day they went to the zoo. The Chinese government had sent a panda on tour. Pandas were something the Chinese were proud of, like we are of our koalas. Pandas don't normally thrive outside China, because they are so happy there, at home. Consequently, according to the newspapers, the panda was off his food. So it would have to be a brief tour. A sign said

GREETINGS! I AM HUNG CHOW *(Ailuropoda melanoleuca)*: PLEASE DO NOT FEED ME!

The special foods — exotic fruits and barks — flown in weekly from the north-western provinces of China were lying in rotting heaps, to which Hung Chow preserved a lofty indifference.

Two Chinese attendants wearing what once were called Mao caps stood there, worried, vigilant.

"That great big bear is a vegetarian!" she said, turning to Kojack. "Supposed to be."

Just then, an international incident occurred. A scrawny, pimply, teenaged boy, goaded by the adolescent croakings of his classmates, chucked something into the panda cage. Pandas are lateral thinkers, playful, clowning, of interest in any zoo fortunate enough to have one. Something lay there in a gaudy red and yellow wrapper. The attendants, too shocked to move, looked at one another in wild surmise.

Moving with a deft lateral motion, playing up to the howls of the crowd, the panda reached out and drew the package into its myopic line of vision. Now the attendants were trying to scale the fence, but, babbling execrations, were getting hung up on the barbed wire.

Custodial hands were laid on the youth.

"It's only a McDonald's burger!" he whined.

Hung Chow stripped the red and yellow skin off the strange fruit that these foreigners had offered him in homage. Exposing the quivering brownish centre. Hmmm . . . Then into the mouth. A sly crinkly grin. It was good. Hung Chow emitted an imperial burp: more!

The crowd at the zoo — mostly divorced men entertaining their weekend daughters with forbidden candy apples — went wild.

Some weeks later two human beings can be seen lunching at Pooh's-in-the-Wood. Their table is heaped with bleaching chicken bones. A beige behemoth crunches more bones under the table. Next to the table rests a silver champagne cooler, containing a spent, inverted bottle of Great Western Brut.

At a nearby table — say, is this quite by accident? — Ursula and Teddy are frowning down into their plates of smoked trout laced with eel. The flinty, straw-coloured riesling in their long-stemmed glasses has hardly been touched. Is this Pandora's best friend among women? Alas! Pandora and Ursula are unable to signal to each other.

Ghostbuster, principal cat of the surgery, along for a rare excursion, wheezes away (full of chicken) on the gentleman's ample lap. Blind Kojack is lecturing Pandora on the human brain — generously including her own. With his curious white cane, carved for him by a Mexican shaman, he makes deft swirling marks on the pavement, as if he were in his old classroom at the medical school.

"The human brain (as you, a medical person, well know) is

divided into two halves. But did you know that one of them — here, this one on the right — is committed to building character and getting the job done, and so forth? In other words, *bor-ing*. But there is the other half, too. We neurologists call this the "Blancmange". It is a precise neurological analogue to life beneath the equator, to life in our own Doreen, also known as the City of the Long Lunch. This half causes all the trouble, because it can't be fully civilised.

"It's like...do you remember the story of Penelope? She would weave at her loom all day, supposedly to keep her suitors at bay, and to keep her mind off them, until her husband Ulysses returned from the Trojan Wars. But every night she would unravel her day's work on what was meant to be her new wedding garment.

"Now this has long been misread as her virtuous attempt to frustrate the suitors. Actually, she was *prolonging* their courtship!

"She was a woman whose name was synonymous with virtue. But at night her Blancmange, the left side of her brain, got to work. It took her husband Ulysses — who was detained while he was romancing various witches — ten years to make it back. Penelope must have been getting no younger, but the suitors were *still there* pressing their claims.

"So you see, my dear girl, uh...uh...gasp, gasp..."

Choke, gasp, rattle rattle. His dirty old man's emphysema flares up again.

Pandora just can't help it. The old tune just hums away like a chiming, unisoned voice-over in her ambivalent little brain. Correction — her Blancmange:

> *"There's lots of wonderful things to eat*
> *and marvellous games to play!*
> *Today's the day the Panda-bears have*
> *Their..."*

MOON-MOUNTAINS

When some of us die, my father claims, we can expect to take a quick trip there, to those Pale Mountains, just above the Murphean Promontory. Though it will be literally the Moon, it will be very like *terra australis* for me, but for my father it will remind him of an Army Air Force Base near Butte, Montana.

But he will never die, *surely my father will never die!*

There are vine-leaves covering the pergola when he breaks the news that he *will* pass — maybe — but that will be insignificant, since he won't pass away from everything, only the mundane. He will enter the Lunar Sphere. He can tell us no more about it right now: arrangements are still being made, bribes and munificents crossing pale argentine palms. But the time will come when the things he had dreamt — for he had dreamt so many remarkable things on this earth — would be exchanged for the things he had surrendered already down below.

Out here this evening among the insect-cries — gossamer creatures caressing our electronic lure, then the horrific wing-blast spiral to our pavement — we are awaiting the nightly light-show, Halley's Comet. We have been at this for as many nights as my father has been with us (recently come down from the North). The comet will pass through the Southern Cross, slightly to the south-east of us. The Moon herself is Piscean this evening. She — I still call the Moon ''she'' — is floating in her circumambient ethers, buoyant as a dandelion-fluff harlot or damasked prima ballerina. We take another pull on our dark-stemmed wineglasses and contemplate this Piscean Moon, as she sails bravely between two cusps of bursting muscat grapes.

Deep in the shadows Alaric is contemplating another Antarctic voyage, part of his struggle . . .

He too is taking a bearing on the moon: for him a sexless and inhuman orb.

My Anne-Marie is silent, as ever, as if moonstruck. I sit where I can see them glisten, those wonderful eyes filled with the moonlight!

My wife, on the other hand, is bustling to and fro, bringing us delicious chocolate things from the microwave oven. My wife, my mainstay down here, down below . . .

As we savour the half-darkness of a sultry evening, my father expatiates, patiently, as if endowed with infinite expanses of time in which to speak, on first and last things.

And my thoughts are taking their own flight — for I am not my father's son for nothing.

We were, all of us, together once before, in the City. In the City, some ways to the south of here, it is regarded as shameful, cowardly, not to act upon the obscure promptings of desire. There I met Anne-Marie for the first time. The people of that City wore all the complexions of the mortal palette. Some say there are six colours of mortal skin, and that all others are blends. Anne-Marie is one of these blends, and I another.

And Alaric, whom we also stumbled upon there, another, darker blend.

This is the City where night after night the addicts prowl the streets looking for money, killing strangers, or, if there be any moon at all, first taking them sexually by force. With a little luck, if you dare to walk these streets at night, you are only beaten and robbed. Cities have lives of their own, surpassing Empires, which only arise and pass away. The cities remain, becoming more and more cosmopolitan, approaching closer and closer their goal, which seems to be to concentrate on one extra-temporal site all the fabled malefactions of mankind.

Alaric's unusual physical aspect was perhaps what recommended him to our prolonged gaze, Anne-Marie and me, arm in arm walking the Martyrstrasse, wearing motley carnival costume, just as the sun was beginning to make its way into the eastern haze.

He had not been abnormal at birth, he assured us, at first, as we sat with him in the Tower of Rats Charmed by Music, a little bistro just off the most respectable of the truly dangerous boulevards. The bistros stay open and this is what keeps us at our streetside table, hour after hour into the dawn, observing the curious beings who are still up and about at all hours.

Ravel's "Rhapsodie Espagnole" was the background music for this scene, burping out of the loudspeakers. My chair was cocked at an angle so that I could hear it better. My eyes still on the street. Without music, where are our souls?

My father, that time, had gone to bed early. He had a big business day ahead of him. A few great companies were going to change hands, we could tell that. But there was no point in asking. We would read about it in the early afternoon tabloids.

Written on the wall, right across from us:

BURN TABLOIDS RESTORE PURE DESIRE

When Alaric was born, he claims, he had a distended brain and head. So much was the brain enlarged that it protruded along the line of the cranium, almost to the point of *pseudoencephaly*.

"My whole brain was...uh...more or less everted, and rested on the top of my cranium. Rather like a wig, you might say. My parents saw to it that I received medical attention for this."

He said this with a wry laugh. As if that would excuse his trying to cadge money out of us, the rich foreigners.

Like the philistine who claps rather too loud and long after an aria, I naively encouraged Alaric both in his lying and in his frankness. This would be the keynote of our association. No lie would remain unspoken or truth withheld between us. But Anne-Marie would be no party to this treaty. She remained a secret to us both.

Anne-Marie was beautiful. Well — to us. The lower jaw tended, perhaps for an unknown observer from a dwindling point in space, towards *agnathia*. But these are details which do not affect materially the whole. An abnormal heredity acting together with a haphazard collision of environmental factors can produce inhibited growth in certain areas. This is unimportant. The point is, she was good company when she was not taciturn. She was even good company when she was in foul spirits. Let's face it — she could do no wrong. We, soon to become and then to remain her closest friends, knew why she chose not to smile, not to marry.

Another wall said:

MARRY BURN ABOLISH PURE DESIRE

I met my second wife in the City, the girl in the chocolate shop where we used to linger, Anne-Marie, Alaric and I. We married on pure impulse. It was only after this that Alaric confessed she was his sister. He had not wanted to influence my choice of wife by any such confidences. My father highly approved of her. He had feared I would marry Anne-Marie herself.

Marry Anne-Marie!

My father had also preferred my first wife to our divine Anne-Marie. His tastes were formed in another era, and in the fastnesses of the mountains. My first wife, Rowena, would, for years after the divorce, jet in sometimes, just for a little legal skirmishing, and my father would be there at the Drome, nasturtia in hand.

Not a pretty sight, a father doting on one's ex-wife! She had no father of her own and relished his attentions. I found out later, after receiving a nasty drubbing in the courts, that my father's money had been behind her. Since of course at law it is merely a matter of who can buy the best lawyers, she always won. So that was that. There was her considerable inheritance and then there was that doting old fool, the man who fathered me. But the old fools will always have the jump on the novices.

PURE DESIRE WILL MAKE US WISER
ABOLISH ALL MEDIATED DESIRE

I was reading the graffiti, and thinking, that time in the City, about the origins of my father, and thus, somehow, about the origins of an entirely different being — myself.

He came from a mountainous region bounded on the north by Canada, on the east by North and South Dakota. On the west by... Never mind!

These mountain people worshipped two substances: gold and silver (*Oro y Plata* was inscribed on britches and T-shirts). If they longed for the moon herself, this was because they thought she was a huge ball of, in autumn, the former, in spring the latter.

The Ponderosa pine hung darkly over their heads, obscuring the mountains, so that they never got a clear view of them, and the bitterroot flower clung to their spurs as they tried, having first tethered their winded animals to the yellow trunks, to climb beyond the horse-tracks. So — most of them stayed low-down, loafed around at the lower altitudes and took to watching the silver-haired women and golden-haired girls cross the steep streets of the town, towards the ice-cream parlour located at the very heart of the town they called Cancer Gulch.

Is that why my father was inclined to measure beauty by a different benchmark to my own? Because he could never get a clear view of the mountaintops? Men climbing those mountains would die of exhaustion only halfway up the sides. Others would stumble, fall babbling in terror into sudden ravines.

The women of the town of Cancer Gulch were all nominally beautiful — they had to be. The ones deemed ugly, the dark-haired ones, fled or were propelled East or West, to the great universities, where they stood a better chance of signing a marriage contract.

The others, the gold and silver beauties who remained behind, were dressed by their men in the furs of beaver, muskrat, mink, skunk and weasel — all those animals which, while alive, are the most noisome.

This explains a lot, I think, about my father. I remember my mother as a blonde, pink-cheeked confection in dead weasel.

"Mama" died before her hair turned silver, and my father began a life of womanising, to which I was an unwillling adjunct. I would often lie huddled in a snowbank along some frozen bank of Flirt Creek or the Big Blackfoot, Poontang, Big Horn, Clark's Fork, Rosebud, Tongue, or Powder River, while, in some smoky shanty, my father conducted one of his peripatetic amours. Then, just when I had nearly frozen to death, he would burst from the cabin and take me up again on horseback, or later in his Buick, and bear me off homewards. While I slept, at last blissfully warm. Such was my early life with him, before he got rich simply by incarnating one or another of his many dreams.

"You should be careful what you dream," he said once.

The wall said:

TECHNOLOGY WILL NOT ABOLISH PURE DESIRE

Such things about my father, my past, I told Alaric — Alaric the boy who just chanced upon himself one day, alive and kicking, in a ghetto of the City. An object of compassion to the stranger, a cause of heartache to his parents, to his sister.

An object of ridicule to many others. Or so Alaric once said. Now he breaks the silence, breaks into my reverie, reminding me of our current vigil:

"*Hermaphrodites,* as individuals, containing both functioning testes and ovaries, probably do not occur in higher mammals and man, in which the sex is determined by the fertilised ovum and is fundamentally sharply distinct at birth."

Is Alaric making a confession, or what?

We raise our glasses again under the vines of my pergola. It is an ancient, heavily mortgaged stone villa here in the suburbs. We have had a good dinner and now the notion is that we are awaiting

Halley's Comet, due to pass through the Southern Cross at midnight, 35 degrees south of east and 85 degrees from the horizon.

But we are thinking of where we will be *next* time the Comet pays a visit. None of us, it is agreed, will be in what we call "life". But my father claims we will all be somewhere and the implication is, we had better be making our arrangements. Soon it will be too late for bookings in the best places. The Pale Moon-Mountains above the Murphean Promontory are evidently still available. My father is ready to plant a family colony there, in the lunar otherworld.

Politely, we are considering the idea, or pretending to. Alaric has not been invited. Nor has Anne-Marie.

These are the people you will not see again.

The wall had said:

LET MY LOVER BECOME PURE DESIRE

And Alaric is evidently pursuing his own vagrant thoughts:

"Multiple abnormalities trace to a common source in a retardation in early development which in most cases — harelip, contractures, *spina bifida* and mental aberration — is probably due to a defective . . ."

"Oh will you shut up, Alaric!" says Anne-Marie.

Meanwhile my father is continuing his own ultramundane speculations. We will watch the next Comet from the moon, from the summit of the Pale Mountains, is that the idea? And Mama will be in attendance, too, no doubt? Wearing her skunkskin, eh?

But my father is reading my mind, as always:

"It's a lot better than redistributing matter and erasing history — isn't it?"

Alaric has been courting danger (dangerous substances, dangerous actions) for years, trying to do just that.

ERASE HISTORY REDISTRIBUTE MATTER

My friend Alaric doesn't think he wants — *his* — matter to remember itself. He is getting impatient for the Gulf of Mawson, Antarctica. Down there he is not an oddity: they call him Radioman.

Monteverdi (can it really be *Orfeo* we are hearing?) is the background music now, filtering through the French doors that open onto our garden. Music helps us to attain to pure desire.

TECHNOLOGY WILL NOT ABOLISH...

Alaric starts humming one of the arias. We are all reading one another's minds, for he just then cries out:

"It *is Orfeo*! 'La Primavera!'"

And my father is droning on. Only the music of philosophy is in his voice, his thoughts. "And what if on this particular evening the comet does not choose to come?"

"I have never been on an *absolute* mountaintop before: neither in the Highwoods, the Bearpaws, the Beartooths, the Absarokas, the Snowys, or the Little Rockies. Nor could you even *see* them. Those damned yellow Ponderosas some of them *five hundred feet high* always got in the way. And when you got closer you got lost. Nobody I knew of ever got up there and came back. The peaks were only something they put on the maps: little dotted lines marking the...what did we call it?...the Great Divide."

Some of us are only thinking: Can *Orfeo* be ending with such sweet harmony? And will it end the same way as before?

My wife brings out some of her homemade chocolates, my father's favourites. Anne-Marie and Alaric have now both fallen silent. They will be staying in the spare room until Alaric sets off on the voyage southwards. Antarctica. What then? What *could* come after Antarctica? So there is no plan for meeting again, between them, or between us. My father will be going north. Anne-Marie returns to the City.

Our friendship is breaking up in this world. We can't even put this off until the end. We can't leave anything up to accident.

Still we do not go inside, do not refuse this night.

My father has withdrawn slightly from the group, speaking in a low murmur to my wife, who stands there with her tray held vertical, like a shield.

I know I will never see my father again.

Unless he's right.

Unless he really is able to use his influence in the highest places . . .
Quite a funny thought, if so.

We wheel our chairs around, dividing the freshly turned loam.
We wheel them around, one by one to face the south. The Southern
Cross is astonishingly bright between the electric wires.

Midnight.

And now we all turn together to watch it, a dim funnel-web of
light, like an imperfection in some zone of the eye.

Slowly, it is not imagination, it is the Visitor, the Wanderer.
It is Halley's Comet.

Passing to the region of pure desire.